J
DEW

DeWeese, Gene *Cop1* *6/87*

The dandelion caper

$13.95

DATE			

THE DANDELION CAPER

THE
DANDELION
CAPER

Gene DeWeese

G. P. PUTNAM'S SONS / NEW YORK

Library of Congress Cataloging-in-Publication Data
DeWeese, Gene. The dandelion caper.
Summary: Having rescued many stranded "tourists" from outer space, Walter and his
friend Kathy are unprepared for the evil aliens they encounter in an abandoned house
and the strange cat with unusual powers that comes to their rescue.
[1. Science fiction. 2. Cats—Fiction] 1. Title.
PZ7.D522Dan 1986 [Fic] 86-8137
ISBN 0-399-21326-0
First impression

For the original Dandelion,
who wasn't around nearly long enough

CONTENTS

THE DANDELION CAPER

1

"Maybe We Better Not Bother Them."

I used to figure that if creatures from outer space ever really did come visiting, it would just naturally be the biggest thing that ever happened to Earth. I mean, either they'd wipe us out altogether or they'd invite us into some kind of galactic federation, and you can't get much bigger than that.

But that was before I met a bunch of them. For one thing, they didn't even *have* a galactic federation, as far as I could tell. For another, they were almost as klutzy as I am, which is saying quite a bit.

At least the one my best friend Kathy Entsminger and I rescued from Sheriff Pippenger was. He was a sort of undercover tourist, just like all the others we met, and he didn't even know what *star* he was from, for crying out loud! He even managed to mislay his rented spaceship, and if that wasn't enough, the gadget that kept him looking more or less human broke down, which meant he couldn't even go out in public and *look* for his ship without scaring people half to death or getting shot at. All he could do was stay out of sight while Kathy and I scrounged around and found his ship and brought it back to him.

All of which was exciting enough, don't get me wrong. Just the idea that he was from another solar system who-knows-how-many light-years away and that there were tons of others just like him, wandering around all over Earth, did sort of give me goose bumps. It's just that nothing was quite the way it *should've* been. I mean, who would've thought that people who can hop around from star to star like that would be klutzes?

I guess what it really amounts to is, no matter where they're from or what they look like, they're not a whole lot smarter than we are. They just have a lot of super-scientific gadgets that we don't. Gadgets, for instance, that let them disguise themselves—and their ships—so they look like people or rocks or cats or who knows what else.

The trouble is, they don't have the foggiest idea how those gadgets work, or how to fix them when they *quit* working. They just use them, the same way we use *our* gadgets. And you know what it's like when one of *them* conks out, like your TV set or your car, and all you know how to do is change channels or check the air in the tires. It's the same for people from outer space, only more so. For one thing, their gadgets are even harder to understand than ours.

What's worse, they don't have any repair shops here on Earth, which is something they definitely need if the gadgets that first bunch had are any example. They seem to break down every time you so much as look cross-eyed at them, no matter how superscientific they are.

But that's probably pretty lucky for us, especially for Kathy and me, and maybe for the rest of the world too. I mean, not *everybody* that comes here from outer space is going to be a harmless tourist.

This new bunch we ran into, for instance, weren't all that harmless, not by a long shot. I mean, they acted like real intergalactic nasties, and they came awfully close to doing us in, no questions asked. If it hadn't been for Uncle Harold and my little brother Walter— and Dandelion, of course, not to mention their own klutziness and their bargain-basement equipment and a few other things—I really don't think Kathy and I would be around to start the seventh grade this fall at good old Vernon J. Dalhart Middle School.

But I'm getting ahead of myself, which is what Kathy is always warning me about. "You're so logical, Mr. Spock," she says, "so start at the logical place—at the beginning."

She calls me that every so often, which I don't really mind, since Mr. Spock is kind of my ideal, the way he looks at everything logically. Sort of like my dad, but with pointy ears and without the crew cut Dad and I both have. (That hair of Spock's, by the way, is the one thing that makes me wonder now and then if he's really as logical as he makes out to be. Like Dad always says, a crew cut's the only logical kind of haircut to have unless you happen to enjoy messing around with a comb and all that spray stuff they have now.) Dad's an engineer, by the way, a microchip designer, which is maybe why he's always been pretty logical and all that. I mean, all those schematics and logic diagrams and things will do that to you, or at least that's what Mom says. But then, Mom's a little like Kathy. They both work pretty much on intuition, whatever that is. Hunches, I guess.

Before I forget it, my name's Calvin Willeford, which, unfortunately, sort of fits me, what with my general klutziness and my glasses and the fact that no matter how much food, junk and otherwise, I stuff myself with, I still don't weigh a lot more than Kathy, even if I am four or five inches taller.

But like I started to say, the beginning *this* time was Friday, about a week and a half after Kathy and I located that tourist's spaceship for him and then got him away from Sheriff Pippenger so he could head back to wherever he came from. That was when we biked out to the old Diefenbacher place, where we figured we'd be sure to run into some more aliens. We'd planned to go out there the weekend before, but what with bad weather and studying for final exams, that was the first chance we had.

See, we were both pretty sure that the guy who had been trying to buy the place from Mom (she works for a real-estate company a couple of days a week) was mixed up with those outer-space tourists one way or another. Since it's such an out-of-the-way place, five or six miles outside town on a back road, we figured the tourist agencies were going to use it to park their interstellar tour busses while they let the tourists wander around observing us "natives." (Town, by the way, is East Gradwohl, which isn't really all that logical a name, since there isn't any *West* Gradwohl.)

Anyway, Kathy was getting so impatient by then that she was ready to pedal out there whether it stopped raining or not, which was sort of understandable. When we finally got there, though, it was something of a letdown. I mean, if the Diefenbacher place really was being taken over by aliens, you couldn't tell it by looking. It still looked pretty much the same way it had a couple of weeks before, when Mom had driven Walter and me and Dad past the place just after she'd sold it. The weeds were so thick in the long lane that led up from the road that we had to walk our bikes, only now the ground was soaking wet from the rain we'd had the last few days, which didn't do our sneakers any good at all. We were both squishing by the time we got to the front yard and leaned our bikes against a couple of trees. The yard was just as thick with weeds as the lane, and half the windows in the house were boarded up or broken, just like before.

"Well," I said, "what now?"

"The logical thing would be to see if anyone's home," Kathy said, more than a little sarcastically. Not that I could blame her. It *had* been a sort of dumb question, considering we'd ridden five or six miles and pushed the bikes through all those wet weeds to get here.

I followed her up the rickety steps to the front door. They creaked, and so did the porch. There were only a few patches of paint left on the door, and of course there wasn't any doorbell. Kathy hesitated all of two or three seconds—which for her is a pretty long time—before knocking.

There wasn't any answer, of course, but there was a noise, sort of. "Squirrels," I said. I'd seen some of them scampering around in the trees. "Or rats."

"Or more aliens," Kathy said, shading her eyes and peering through the window—really grimy—that filled the top half of the door.

After a few seconds, she banged on the door again, and after another few she took hold of the knob.

And turned it.

The door swung open, sounding like something out of a haunted-house movie.

This time it took Kathy even longer, maybe ten or fifteen seconds, before she pushed the door the rest of the way open and stuck her head inside.

"Anybody home?" she yelled.

There wasn't any answer, but I was sure I heard more scrabbling sounds from somewhere farther inside.

"Come on, Calvin," she said, reaching back and grabbing my hand, "let's go."

I held back, but not very much.

It was pretty much like when we'd been out here last summer, which was the last time we'd been all the way inside the abandoned house. Laths showing through the plaster in a couple of places. No furniture. Cobwebs in all the corners. Dust on everything.

The only difference was, we kept hearing those noises every so often, like a dog's toenails on a wood floor. Or sometimes like rats scampering through the walls.

16

"Hear all that stuff?" Kathy said. She couldn't keep the enthusiasm out of her voice. "I bet they're all around us! Invisible!"

I shivered. I'd gotten used to the idea that there were all kinds of weird-looking aliens around East Gradwohl, disguised as people or rocks or whatever, but I guess I still wasn't ready for the idea that they could be disguised as *nothing*, like ghosts.

"Maybe we better not bother them," I said.

"And maybe they're in trouble, like that one that lost his spaceship," Kathy said.

Which was logical enough, I guess, but it didn't help with my shivers, especially when I looked down at the floor and noticed that the dust wasn't all that evenly distributed. There were our own wet footprints, of course, but there was a lot of other stuff too. Not really footprints or anything like that, but streaks, like somebody'd been dragging something around. And here and there were little scratches—claw marks?—in the wood. And the grungy old carpet that was still tacked to the stairway had rips in it.

"Come on," Kathy said after she'd stood perfectly still, listening, for half a minute or so. "It sounds like they're upstairs."

So of course we went upstairs, which turned out to be a hallway with two or three open doors on each side and one at the end. Kathy stood at the head of the stairs, listening again, but this time there wasn't a sound.

"Hey," she said, talking to what I sort of hoped was empty air, "there's nothing to be afraid of. We know all about you. We saved one of your friends last week. A big hairy guy, nine or ten feet tall."

17

She listened again, but there still wasn't a sound. Except for something that could have been the wind, or maybe something breathing.

"And my friend here," she went on, grabbing my hand and holding it up in the air, "he's got one of your beepers. A—a— What was it you called it, Calvin?"

"The guy we rescued called it a milorganite device," I said, and I guess that's something I better explain. It's a big, lumpy ring, and I got it from some other alien, probably a local representative of one of the travel agencies that's been sending all these tourists to Earth and to all the other "backward" planets in the galaxy.

It's sort of a long story, but what it all boils down to is, the ring, like Kathy said, is an outer-space beeper of some kind. It's called a milorganite device, and whenever some nearby tourist needs help or wants to ask a question, he sends out a signal that the ring can pick up. Then the ring makes me sort of tingle, and, somehow or other, it tells me which way to go to find the tourist so I can answer his question or help him or whatever.

At least that's the way it's *supposed* to operate, according to the big hairy guy we rescued. I mean, the ring I have isn't the only one around. There must be hundreds or maybe even thousands of them all over the world, all given out by those intergalactic travel agencies to people they've recruited to be "native guides." All those others might even get paid some way or other, I don't know. The thing is, I got my ring *accidentally*, so I never got anything explained to me, at least not officially, and I'm still not really sure just how far we can trust what that guy we rescued told us.

18

Besides, the ring hadn't done anything since a day or two after I got it, and I was pretty sure that it had just quit working altogether. Like I said, these outer-space gadgets do break down a lot.

But it was still on my finger for Kathy to point at, and she was doing a bang-up job of that.

"That's right," Kathy was saying as she went along the hall, pointing back at me and my finger, "a milorganite device. See? Right there on his finger."

By then she was at the door at the end of the hall, poking her head through and looking around. I was still back at the head of the stairs, and it was about then that I heard something creak.

Something like a stair step.

I jerked around to look down the stairs, but of course there was nothing there. Nothing I could see, anyway.

Twitching a little, I hurried after Kathy, and a second later we were both in the room at the end of the hall. There was only one window, and it looked out over the backyard, which was even more of a jungle than the front. A hundred feet back, some trees looked like they were trapped in a big grapevine twenty or thirty feet wide. Beyond that were some woods, which turned into a swamp after a few hundred yards.

"If you're in trouble," Kathy said to the air, "maybe we can help. Like I said, we know all about you, so you don't have to worry about showing yourself. If you don't—"

The door to the room slammed shut behind us.

Kathy and I both jerked around. Even Kathy looked scared, at least for the moment.

Then there was a click. From the door.

I grabbed at the knob, but it wouldn't turn.

And on the other side of the door there were more noises, only these weren't footsteps or scrapes or clicks. These were voices. High-pitched, squeaky voices that didn't sound even faintly human.

What's worse, they didn't sound anything at all like those tourists we'd run into, either. These sounded like something totally different.

They also sounded upset, very upset.

2

"If Anyone Can Have a Logical Subconscious, It's You."

After a second, Kathy tried the knob, but it wouldn't budge any more for her than it had for me.

"Hey, you guys!" she yelled, banging on the door with her fist. "Quit fooling around! I told you, we know all about you! There's no reason for you to lock us up in here! If you're in trouble, like that big hairy guy was last week, maybe we can help."

"I think this is a different bunch altogether," I said, but Kathy didn't seem to hear me, she was so busy yelling at the door.

"Kathy!" I said, grabbing her arm to get her attention. When she finally looked at me, I repeated what I'd said.

"Different? What's that supposed to mean?" she asked, looking both ticked off and nervous.

"Don't you remember what the other one sounded like when his translation gadget broke down?" I asked her. "Real deep voice with a kind of gargling sound to it? Just listen to these. All they're doing is squeaking. Besides, none of the ones we ran into before tried to lock us up like this."

"You're saying these aren't tourists? That they're spies or something?"

"*I* don't know what they are! But whatever they are, maybe we shouldn't yell at them, just in case."

She looked back at the door. The voices were still squeaking at each other. It was starting to sound like an argument between a couple of rusty hinges.

"Maybe we can get out through the window," Kathy said abruptly, and a second later she was at the room's only window, trying to raise it.

But it wouldn't budge, and you could see it had been painted shut ages ago. Probably the only paint in the house that wasn't peeling and cracking, I thought, and naturally it's blocking our only way out.

Not that it would've made a lot of difference, I decided as I looked through the dirty glass. Without a ladder, there was no way we could've gotten down anyway. There were enough weeds to halfway cushion our fall just about everywhere else, but under the window there was nothing but the cracked concrete of what might've been a patio twenty years ago.

I was, believe it or not, thinking about breaking the window and trying to lower Kathy far enough so she wouldn't break anything when she fell the rest of the way. I guess I figured she could find a ladder or make a big pile of weeds for me to fall on or something.

But by the time I started wondering how I could

break the window and get all the glass out without bleeding all over everything, the argument outside the door stopped. The squeaks just quit, like somebody turned off a radio, and for a second I wondered if maybe it *had* been some kind of radio, not real noises made by real monsters or whatever.

Then there was a click.

It sounded like the door being unlocked, and it all of a sudden occurred to me that maybe the squeaks had quit because the argument had been settled, and now they were coming in to get us.

But the door didn't open.

Kathy went to the door and pressed her ear against it, listening.

Then she took the knob in her hand and turned it.

And swung the door open a crack.

Nothing happened. No sound. Nothing.

She looked out into the hall, and I crowded close, looking over her shoulder. The hall was empty.

But looking down, I could see that the dust was a lot more stirred up than it had been when we'd come in. We'd left some damp footprints, but they were totally gone, wiped out by whatever had been arguing out there.

Kathy stuck her head out through the door and poked at the air with her finger, like she was feeling for the invisibles, which I suppose she was.

Then she opened the door all the way, and we both inched out into the hall. I poked the air, too, and couldn't feel anything. It did smell kind of funny, though. Not so much musty and dusty the way it had before, but sort of yucky damp, like the wind had shifted and was blowing off that swamp a few hundred yards back of the house.

After a few cautious steps down the hall, we quit poking the air and feeling our way along. By the time we reached the stairs a dozen feet away, we were almost running. We galloped down the stairs, raising puffs of dust from the ragged stair carpet.

Downstairs there still wasn't a sound except the echo of our own feet hitting the bare floor, and when we hit the front door, Kathy stopped. I stopped a second later, out on the porch.

We both listened. Still no voices, and none of the dog-claw sounds, or the rats-in-the-walls scratchings, either.

Total silence except for our breathing and the usual stuff outside—a little wind in the trees and a bird or two and a truck somewhere in the distance.

"What happened?" Kathy asked, and I could only shrug.

"Maybe they just had to check out our story," she went on. "Maybe that was a radio we heard, and they were contacting headquarters or their travel agent or something, and he told them we were okay."

"Maybe," I said, but I didn't really think so.

I really hate to admit it, but I had a hunch. Now, that's the kind of thing Kathy and Mom are having all the time, but not me or Dad. But this time I had one. Maybe I've just been hanging around with Kathy too much, and some of whatever she's got has rubbed off on me, I don't know. Or maybe it was just the fact that these aliens had been completely invisible, and not being able to see them at all was making me more nervous than seeing big hairy monsters that I could at least talk to.

Anyway, this hunch or whatever it was told me that the invisibles weren't just another batch of tourists and that it wasn't just a little help they wanted, or a few questions answered.

Kathy, however, was still convinced they *were* just another batch of tourists, only with squeaky voices and a sort of swamp-sweat odor. She was even starting to think about going back inside, believe it or not. So, much as I hated to do it, I told her about my hunch.

To my total surprise, she didn't laugh. "It's probably your subconscious," she said, and when I looked blank she went on. "There's probably some logical reason for you to think what you're thinking, but your conscious mind just hasn't noticed it yet, that's all. But your subconscious has, and I'll bet it's just as logical as the rest of you, so maybe it's right." She paused and grinned a little. "If anyone can have a logical subconscious, it's you. So maybe we'd better get out of here after all."

So back we went into the wet weeds and picked up our bicycles. We were starting to walk them out of the yard when I saw Dandelion. That is, I saw a cat. I didn't know it was Dandelion at the time, or anything else.

It was sitting on a low branch of one of the trees, the same one where I'd seen the squirrels on the way in. It was very long-haired and very yellow, with some darker areas that were sort of orangeish. Its tail, almost as bushy as a squirrel's, was wrapped around it so that it looked like it was sitting on a big, fuzzy, golden cushion. Even its eyes were yellow, and they were watching us like it thought we were a couple of large birds.

Kathy saw it a second or two after I did.

"Calvin!" she said, pointing. "That isn't the cat that gave you the ring, is it?"

I shook my head as I leaned my bike against another tree. Kathy just let hers flop over in the weeds.

"That one was gray and plain and kind of fuzzy-looking," I said, "like the tourists. Besides, it wasn't a cat, it was someone from the local branch of their tourist agency *disguised* as a cat, and it didn't *give* me the ring, it dropped it when Hulk jumped it and I threw water on them to break the fight up." Hulk, by the way, is my twenty-pound tiger stripe. Normally he's pretty placid, except when he wants to play, but that alien disguised as a cat must've smelled funny or something, which is probably the only reason Hulk jumped it the way he did.

"Maybe this is just a better disguise," Kathy said, eyeing the cat.

It was possible, I supposed, and I moved closer to the tree. As I got within a few feet, the cat stood up on the branch, its tail sticking straight up like a bushy flagpole. As it stood up, I could see that it had the shortest legs of any cat I'd ever seen, although I realized a second later that this was partly an illusion, caused by the fact that its hair was so long that only an inch or two of leg stuck out underneath it.

"If it's a real cat, at least it's friendly," Kathy said.

"That's how they hold their tails when they like you."

"I know," I said. I'd seen Hulk that way often enough, especially just before meals, which was usually when his friendliness hit a peak.

I could just barely reach the branch by standing on tiptoes and stretching. When I did, the cat backed away, its tail still in the air. I scratched on the bottom of the branch with my fingernail and made a clicking noise with my tongue against my teeth. That kind of thing usually worked with Hulk, but this one didn't pay any attention. Or rather, it didn't move any closer. It was still watching every move I made, from three or four feet away on the branch.

"Maybe it can't get down," Kathy said. "Cats have more trouble getting out of trees than they have getting up in them."

"It doesn't look very worried," I said.

Then, on an impulse, I put both hands up and jumped, catching the limb and trying to pull myself up. All I managed to do, though, was chin myself and realize that there was no way I was going to hook my leg over the branch and get the rest of the way up.

But then, just as I was about to lower myself and let go, I felt something cold on one of my fingers, and I heard Kathy laugh. I looked around, and there was the cat, about five inches from my face, its cold nose sniffing at my hand.

Or, to be more exact, it was sniffing at the finger that had the ring on it.

For a second, I thought I was in real trouble, that maybe this *was* another alien disguised as a cat, and it was going to start clawing at me any second, or zapping me with something, or maybe taking the ring back.

But it didn't claw me or zap me or anything else. It just sniffed and gave me the kind of look Hulk gives me when he's expecting some special treat for lunch.

"Here," Kathy said, "I'll hold you up. You see if you can grab it."

And before I could say anything, I felt Kathy grabbing me around the knees and lifting. "Hurry up," she said. "You're skinny, but I can't hold you up forever."

So I let go of the branch, at least with one hand, and reached for the cat with the other. It backed away, of course.

But then, after another yellow-eyed stare, it darted forward, hopped off the branch onto my shoulder, ran head first down my back onto Kathy's shoulder, and jumped the rest of the way to the ground.

Kathy dropped me, of course, and turned to follow the cat.

But it didn't go very far. It went fifteen or twenty feet, to where I'd leaned my bicycle against a tree. By the time I picked myself up, it seemed to be studying the bicycle, and after another second or two it hopped up and climbed into the big wire basket on the front. The bike wobbled and slipped a little, but somehow it didn't fall over.

Then the cat sat down, curled its tail around itself again, and just watched us, but with a very expectant look on its face.

Like it knew something was going to happen and was just waiting to see what it was.

3

"The Hulk-and-Walter Test."

Kathy must've been thinking the same thing I was, because she looked over her shoulder toward the house about the same time I did, like we were expecting whatever the cat was waiting for to come running out.

But nothing happened. No more noises or voices or anything, and nothing came running out. Nothing visible, anyway.

So we looked back at the cat. It was still sitting in my bicycle basket, watching us. Or watching me, at any rate.

"You're *sure* that's not the cat that gave you the ring?" Kathy asked, sounding skeptical.

"Absolutely," I said as we edged closer. If there ever was a cat that didn't look like the one I got the ring from, this was it. And it wasn't just the fact that this one was fluffy and yellow while the other had been short-haired and a sort of all-purpose

The main difference was, this one looked *real*. Up close, you could see every whisker and every hair, including the longest ear tufts I'd ever seen. They were like silky tendrils, almost as long as its whiskers. The markings were very distinct, too, an odd pattern of dark and light, ranging from a sort of orange to an almost dandelion yellow, which is why I started thinking of it by that name right about then. At least I think that's why, but I wouldn't bet on it. That was also when I started thinking of it as a her, and I didn't have any logical reason for *that* either.

Anyway, despite her run through the weeds, she still looked perfectly groomed, almost like she'd been blow-dried. And she had a collar. It was hidden by her lionlike ruff, but once we got close enough we could see it.

"She belongs to someone," I said. "See the collar? I bet that's why she jumped into my basket. It's a trick her owner taught her."

"I didn't think you could teach a cat *anything*," Kathy said doubtfully, but she didn't say anything about the fact that I'd started calling the cat "she." I guess she'd started thinking about her that way, too.

"You can't," I said, remembering one of Dad's lines when I'd first found Hulk and was trying to train him to use the litter box, "unless it's something they want to learn in the first place."

By this time, we were right next to my bike, and I reached out to try to scratch behind Dandelion's ears, which, along with food, was something Hulk could never get enough of. At first she drew back, but after a few seconds she must've decided she liked it. She sat up

30

a little straighter, and the tip of her tail began to twitch in time with the scratching.

"She sure *feels* like a real cat," I said.

Kathy shrugged. "If she is, we better look at the collar. Maybe there's a name on it."

But there wasn't any tag, and as far as we could see there wasn't anything written on the collar itself. For a while, I couldn't even find a buckle, and when I finally did it had some kind of trick catch I couldn't open. Kathy didn't have any better luck than I did.

As for Dandelion, she just sat there in the basket, putting up with all our experimenting, watching every move we made.

Finally, cautiously, I took the bicycle away from the tree and started walking it through the weeds toward the road. I figured she'd jump out at the first bump, and if I wanted to take her home I'd have to go get a cat carrier or have Mom pick her up in the car, like she did with Hulk last year.

But Dandelion didn't budge. She just settled down, folding her front feet in under her ruff and wrapping her tail halfway around herself again.

Out on the road, I climbed on and started pedaling, very slowly at first. I was still half expecting her to jump out, and I didn't want to be going so fast she'd hurt herself.

But she still didn't budge. She just lay there, watching everything we went past, occasionally turning her head and looking up at me. Even when we got out on the highway, which we have to take for a mile or so just south of town, she stayed calm. Calmer than me a couple of times, like when a semi came whizzing past and practically knocked us over with the wind it made.

When we got home, Mom was making her version of a TV dinner, a sort of meat-and-vegetable casserole that we can just stick in the oven and heat up on evenings when she's been selling houses all day and doesn't feel like making anything new. As usual, it looked—and sounded—like she was having trouble with the electronic timer on the oven.

"Just what is it," she was muttering to herself as we hesitated just outside the screen door, "that you blankety-blank microchips have against me, anyway? What did *I* ever do to *you?*"

Which, maybe I should explain, is the sort of thing you hear around our place quite a bit, and not just from Mom. I mean, Dad designs all sorts of things using microchips out at Harding Microelectronics where he works, and he's really gung ho about that sort of thing. He's always finding some new electronic whatchamacallit in the stores, a new watch that tells you when it's high tide in Timbuktu or a gadget you can hang on your keychain that will beep at you if you yell at it. He even brings things home from Harding to show off now and then.

The thing is, they break down almost as often as those outer-space gadgets do, and Dad always blames Mom or me or Walter for it. We must've pushed the wrong button or yelled at it the wrong way or something, he says. And it's been that way as long as I can remember. Mom and Walter and I even wear old windup-type watches instead of digital, since none of the digital ones Dad got us ever lasted long enough to run down a battery.

Anyway, after a few more stabs at the oven's buttons, Mom gave up and turned it on by hand and set her old kitchen timer for forty minutes. Then she looked around at the two of us, still peering in through the screen door. Or the three of us, I should say. Dandelion, who had hopped out of the basket almost the second I'd stopped, had trotted up onto the porch with us and was standing up on her hind legs, leaning against the screen and looking through.

"*Where* did you get *that?*" Mom asked, giving us a frown.

"We found her," I said.

"Found it? Where?" she asked, easing herself out through the screen door and joining us on the back steps.

"We were out looking around the Diefenbacher place," I admitted.

Mom frowned. "And what were you doing out *there?*"

"Just looking around," Kathy put in. "You know, before that Mr. Johnson that's buying the place puts up 'No Trespassing' signs."

"I don't suppose you *saw* Mr. Johnson?"

"We didn't see *anybody,*" Kathy said. "Why?"

"I was just hoping, I guess," Mom said, shaking her head. "He seems to have vanished."

"I thought you said he brought the money in last week," I said. "I thought everything was settled."

"I thought everything was, too. He brought in the total amount—in cash—just the way he said he would. It's in the office safe. The trouble is, that's the last anybody's seen of him. He was going to come back in two or three days, once we had time to get all the papers ready for signing, but he never showed up. I even went out to the Diefenbacher place myself and looked around a couple of days ago, hoping I'd find him. Or find *something*." She shook her head again. "If he doesn't show up next week, I'm going to have someone check that money to see if it's counterfeit, in which case this whole thing has just been a bad joke."

"I'm sorry, Mrs. Willeford," Kathy said, and for a second I was afraid she was going to start telling Mom about the squeaky voices and all the rest of the stuff out at the Diefenbacher place. But she didn't, any more than she'd told anyone about how we rescued the tourist. Like me, she knew nobody'd believe us.

"Thank you, Kathy," Mom said, "but that's all right. Now, about this cat—"

"She was in a tree in front of the house," I said. "I'll bet someone dumped her out there, just like they did Hulk."

"With a collar?" Mom asked, leaning down to look more closely.

"Maybe she's just lost. And we already looked at the collar. There's no name on it."

"How did you get her here? You're certainly not going to tell me she followed you all that way, are you?"

"That's the weird part, Mom. She just hopped into my bicycle basket and stayed there. Whoever owned her must've trained her that way."

"And that's probably how she got lost, too," Mom said with a frown. "Someone took her out for a ride, and she jumped out."

"I suppose," I said. "But what should we do? Put an ad in the lost and found?"

"That sounds eminently reasonable," she said, which was one of Dad's favorite lines, one Mom uses every so often, too, usually whenever one of us says something that's sort of obvious, like when she picks up the phone and Dad looks up and says something like "You going to call somebody?" That kind of thing.

"You better let her inside, though," Kathy said, "so she won't run away before you find out who she belongs to."

"The garage—" Mom began, but Kathy interrupted.

"She'd get all dirty," she said, and then I realized why she wanted Dandelion in the house. Hulk. If Hulk didn't object to her, that meant she was probably a regular cat. If he did, if he reacted the way he had when that imitation cat had showed up, then there was a pretty good chance that she wasn't really a cat at all.

In the end, Mom relented, and she opened the screen door a little warily. Dandelion darted in immediately, her tail still upright.

And Hulk, who had been watching proceedings through the screen of an open window in the next room, came galloping in. Kathy and I pretty much held our breath, and for a second I wished I'd thought to get a glass of water before the door had been opened.

But we didn't need one.

Hulk came to a sudden stop only inches from Dandelion. Instead of hissing or growling or jumping on her, he just stuck his nose way out and sniffed, like he does with the feet of some human that comes in the

35

house for the first time. Dandelion didn't do anything, just stood there, enduring the inspection.

Then, to everyone's surprise, Hulk took another step forward until he was right in front of her, looming over her like a tank over a jeep.

And he started to wash her, his big tongue slurping away at her head and ears.

I gave Kathy a look, which she returned with a small shrug. That seemed to settle the question of whether Dandelion was a real cat or not, and when my seven-year-old brother Walter came trooping in from playing with some other little kids across the street, it was settled even more. See, whenever Walter was around one of those aliens, he sort of sensed them, only he didn't know what was happening and it scared him.

But with Dandelion there wasn't the least bit of a reaction, except his usual reaction to *any* new animal, which is to pick it up and pet it. Or, if he can't manage both at once, to just pet it. So far he's never managed to get all four of Hulk's feet off the floor at one time, but he had no trouble with Dandelion, who was less than half Hulk's size, even with all the hair.

As for Dandelion, she seemed to take it rather well. Much better, in fact, than most cats Walter tries it on. She didn't struggle at all, and even seemed to be enjoying it, particularly when he gave her a few scratches behind the ears. We never did hear her purr, though, but lots of cats don't, at least not loud enough to hear unless you put your ear right next to them.

Anyway, that really clinched it for Kathy. Never mind that we'd found Dandelion at the Diefenbacher place. Never mind that she acted sort of strange, even for a cat. She *must* be a cat or else she couldn't have passed the Hulk-and-Walter test.

The first thing we did once Mom decided we could leave Dandelion in the house was dig out a spare litter pan, just in case she didn't want to share one with Hulk, for which no one could possibly blame her. She looked at it, sniffed at it a little, and headed back upstairs out of the basement and proceeded to explore every room in the house, which is pretty much what most cats will do when they're in a strange house. Hulk certainly did when he came inside the first time. Walter, of course, followed her every step, petting her or scratching behind her ears whenever she stood still long enough, just the way he'd done with Hulk. Every couple of minutes he'd come running back to report on whatever new things she'd gotten into.

Once the exploration was over, I tried introducing her to Hulk's scratching post in the living room. It's one of the large-economy-size models, like Hulk, about four feet tall. (Anything smaller he'd just knock over.) Dandelion, however, didn't want anything to do with it. She just looked and walked away. Just for the safety of the furniture, then, Mom decided I'd better take a look at her claws and see if they needed clipping. I do Hulk's every few weeks, just enough to keep them from being so sharp and pointy they catch in the rug and trip him, which is what used to happen when I first got him.

But when I looked at Dandelion's paws—which, to my surprise, she let me do without a single objection— I saw I wouldn't have to worry about clipping her claws. She didn't have any. It looked like she'd been declawed, which Mom always thought was carrying things a little too far. (I know, the fact that she didn't have any claws should've been a tipoff that, no matter what the results of the Hulk-and-Walter test, there was still something fishy about her. After all, she'd gotten up into that tree we'd found her in *somehow*. It's the sort of thing Kathy would've picked up on right away, but she'd left for home once she was convinced Dandelion wasn't another alien tourist and therefore couldn't answer any worthwhile questions.)

Anyway, by the time Dad got home, Dandelion was pretty much a member of the family. Mom, however, was still insisting that we put a "Lost and Found" classified in the *East Gradwohl Gazette*, even if she was a little ticked off at the owners for having had the cat declawed.

Then it was suppertime, and it was my turn to try to keep Hulk from climbing my leg while I opened a can of cat food. Dandelion, back from her latest explorations, sat under the kitchen table, watching me intently. From the way Mom was looking at her and commenting about how "well behaved" the cat was and how maybe she'd be a "good example" for Hulk, it looked like she was starting to hope that nobody answered the "Lost and Found" ad.

Hulk of course dived into his food the instant his dish hit the floor, without any preliminary sniffing or anything. As far as we've been able to tell, his only requirement for food is that it can be chewed and swallowed, rapidly, and I'm not so sure he always worries all that much about chewing. He wouldn't resurface until every last crumb was gone and the dish virtually polished.

Dandelion was another matter, at least at first. She began by sniffing at the dish, just about the way she'd done with the litter pan. Then she half turned around, like she was going to walk away, but instead she looked toward Hulk, who was crouched possessively over his own dish, sucking up the contents like an industrial-strength vacuum cleaner.

For ten or fifteen seconds, she watched him, then glanced around at Mom and Walter and me. Finally she turned back to her own dish. Her nose twitched, like she didn't think much of what she was smelling, but then she crouched down over it and got even fluffier-looking than usual. The way her ruff blossomed out, you couldn't even see the dish. But two or three minutes later, about the time Hulk had finished the absolute last crumb in his own dish and was starting to look around for more, she straightened up, and her dish was as empty as his.

After that, she headed straight for the couch and settled down, her tail wrapped around herself so that it looked almost like she was sitting on her own cushion, just like when I'd first seen her in the tree.

And that was that for a couple of hours, except for Mom and Walter ruffling her fur every so often and scratching behind her ears, which she seemed to enjoy almost as much as Hulk did.

I was up in my room most of the evening, trying to read a paperback about some kid who turned into a nonstandard sort of werewolf every now and then. It wasn't a bad book, but I couldn't keep my mind on it. I kept thinking about alien tourists and those noises we'd heard out at the Diefenbacher place and all the rest, including Dandelion.

Then, a little after eight, the door to my room swung open—I hadn't latched it, I guess—and Dandelion walked in. She gave me a look and hopped up on my bed and settled down, just like she had on the couch earlier. A few seconds later, Hulk came trailing in and hopped up beside her. He looked like he was about to try washing her again, but this time he just walked around her once or twice and then picked another corner of the bed, stretched a couple of times, and curled up and did his tiger-striped-beachball imitation.

And that's when I started to tingle.

It took me a few seconds, but I finally realized what it was. It was the same tingle I'd been getting those first couple of days after I'd gotten the ring. The tingle that meant there was an outer-space tourist in the neighborhood and he wanted to ask me a question about something, about some "quaint Earth custom" or whatever.

Without really thinking, I jumped up from my chair and ran for the phone to call Kathy, but halfway down the stairs I realized I couldn't use the downstairs phone, not with Mom and Dad right there next to it. I turned around and, being as quiet as I could, slipped into their bedroom, where the upstairs extension was.

I picked it up and dialed Kathy's number. Her mother answered the phone, but after a few seconds Kathy came on the line, just about the same time Dandelion poked her head in the door.

"Kathy," I said the second she got on the line, "that ring is working again, the beeper. I'm getting that same tingle again!"

I could hear her voice get all excited. "Where's it telling you to go?" she asked.

And that's when I realized it wasn't telling me to go anywhere. Normally, along with the tingle, there's this weird feeling, a sort of hunch, it feels like, and it tells me which direction to go in to find whoever it is that's activated the beeper.

But this time it was just making me tingle. It wasn't telling me to go *any*where.

When I told Kathy, she let out a whoop.

"That must mean you're already where you're supposed to be!" she said, almost yelling. "Don't you move! I'll be right over!"

4

"You Mean This Sort of Thing Runs in Your Family?"

I'd barely hung up, however, when the tingle went away, and I started wondering if it had *really* been caused by the ring—the milorganite device. Maybe it had just been all that thinking—and worrying—I'd been doing about invisible aliens.

Or maybe, I thought with a shiver, one of the invisible aliens had followed Kathy and me from the Diefenbacher place and had been hanging around watching me and had accidentally triggered the ring.

Or maybe, considering the way the aliens' gadgets seemed to break down all the time, it had just been a malfunction. Maybe the ring had given itself a short circuit or whatever the milorganite equivalent of a short circuit is. Or maybe something else altogether had set it off, like when your electronic garage door goes up when your neighbor tries to change the channel on his TV set.

But anyway, by the time Kathy showed up, the tingle was long gone, and it didn't look like it was coming back.

"You're *sure* it didn't tell you where to go?" she asked.

"I'm sure," I said. "Besides, it only lasted a couple of minutes. It disappeared right after I called you."

"Whoever it was, maybe he just changed his mind. I don't suppose you looked around outside to see if there were any Suits in the neighborhood."

I shook my head, but before I could say anything, Kathy was heading for the front door, telling me to hurry up. The next thing I knew, we were jogging around the block and through the alleys, looking for someone wearing a black suit and a hat, which is something else I suppose I should explain about.

Like I already mentioned, these tourists all have gadgets that make them look more or less human. The only thing is, the gadgets, even when they're not broken down, make the tourists all look alike, with black suits and wide-brimmed hats and sort of shadowy faces. I guess the gadgets are the bargain-basement variety, like the "agency" that supplies them. From what the hairy guy we rescued told us, it's sort of like the travel agencies here on Earth where when the tour bus breaks down, the passengers have to get out and push.

Anyway, all the tourists we'd run into so far looked the same, and we'd started calling them Suits, and now we were jogging around seeing if any of them were in the neighborhood. We didn't find any, although for a second we thought we had, only it turned out to be old Mr. Hagenmeyer from the next block, on his way home from the library, where he spends a lot of his evenings. Until we got close enough to see who it was, I'd forgotten that a few real people actually do wear black suits and hats, although there aren't a lot of them here in East Gradwohl.

Back at the house, Kathy started looking at Dandelion again, which was easy enough, since she was waiting for us at the front door and stuck to us like glue from then on. Occasionally, she'd rub against my ankles, but mostly she just sat around looking alert, like she was waiting for something to happen, which, come to think of it, is pretty much the way she'd looked right from the start. She also still looked too real to be anything *but* a real cat, and Hulk was still trying to wash her now and then. Our only problem was Walter, who would show up every few minutes for another petting session with Dandelion. Dandelion seemed to enjoy it, but Kathy and I had to be pretty careful what we said while he was around.

Finally, though, it got to be Walter's bedtime, but that was about the same time that Mom started giving me those looks that meant she was getting ready to start dropping hints that it was time for Kathy to be getting home. She also tossed in a reminder about the weekend.

"In case you and Kathy are planning something," she said, "don't forget this is the Sunday we'll be going to see Uncle Harold." And then, to Kathy, "You'd be more than welcome to come along, dear."

Kathy, like she always did when Mom invited her along on one of our visits to Uncle Harold's, shook her head. When Mom went back into the living room to watch the rest of the network movie, I sort of grinned.

"Maybe you *should* come along," I said. "We could tell Uncle Harold about the Suits and everything and see what he thinks."

She frowned at me. "He'd think we're nuts, just like everyone else would."

"Maybe not. He ran into some UFOs of his own forty or fifty years ago, according to Mom."

"What?" Kathy's eyes widened in surprise and then narrowed in something else. Probably suspicion. "You mean this sort of thing runs in your family? What happened? And why didn't you tell me about it before?"

"I didn't think of it," I said, beginning to regret I'd thought of it now.

"How could you *forget* something like that? What sort—"

"I didn't forget it, I just didn't think of it, that's all."

"But with everything that happened to us last week, you'd *have* to think about it! I mean, you visit your uncle every month or so, and now you tell me he talked to a bunch of spacemen just like we did—" She was starting to sound more ticked off every second she thought about it.

"But he didn't, not really," I interrupted.

"But you just said he *did!*"

"They weren't real, for crying out loud! He didn't *really* talk to anyone from outer space."

"How do you know? When did this happen, anyway?"

"I don't know. Forty or fifty years ago. It was before he was married. But it doesn't make any difference, because they were all *imaginary!* Hallucinations."

"Who says?"

"*He* says! Uncle Harold says!"

Kathy blinked and frowned. "Calvin Willeford, that doesn't make any sense."

"Don't blame me! I know it doesn't make sense. That's probably why I didn't think of it before."

"Well, you've thought of it now, so tell me what happened."

I sighed. It really *didn't* make any sense, and I was sorry I'd said anything about it, especially to Kathy. "All I know is what Mom told me," I said. "And all *she* knew about it was what *her* dad told *her*."

"So, what did she tell you?"

"She just said that Uncle Harold told his brother—Mom's father, my grandfather—that he'd been contacted by space people. They were from the planet Wisteria or something crazy like that, and they had a 'Message' for everybody on Earth, but they could only speak through Uncle Harold. You know, the kind of junk they have in those UFO magazines."

"What's so crazy about that? Maybe they were missionaries."

"Missionaries?"

"Sure, why not? They have tourists who come here to *look* at the natives, so why not missionaries who come here to 'convert' us? You know, like the ones we used to send to Africa or the South Seas or wherever. What sort of message was it, anyway?"

"Who knows? I guess they never actually gave it to him. They just told him they *had* a message and that they'd give it to him 'when the time is right.' Or something like that. But they never did. And then he realized it was all his imagination, and that was that."

"How did he figure out he'd imagined it?"

"How should I know? He did, that's all."

"And you've never *asked* him? All these times you've gone to see him, you've never even asked him?"

I shrugged. "Dad says it would embarrass him, and besides, what good would it do? I mean, it was forty or fifty years ago, and it never really happened in the first place."

"Calvin Willeford, I'm surprised at you!" Kathy said, sounding like a pint-sized version of Mom when she's caught me doing something dumb. "I suppose I'll have to go with you this Sunday and ask him myself."

And that was that. She went into the living room, where my folks were getting ready to watch the ten-o'clock news, and she told Mom she'd changed her mind and would like to take her up on the invitation to visit Uncle Harold on Sunday.

Mom looked a little doubtful at first, probably because of the sudden way Kathy had changed her mind, but only for a second, and then she was telling her what time we would pick her up Sunday morning.

As Kathy and I walked to the door a few minutes later, she stopped and looked around the hall. "Where's the cat?" she asked, frowning a little.

"Dandelion? I don't know. Why?"

"Ever since I got here, we were almost tripping over her. She was following us everywhere."

Which was true enough. She'd been practically sitting on my feet when we'd been talking about Uncle Harold. "Maybe she finally went down to the litter pan," I said.

But when we went down to look, she wasn't there.

47

Hulk had been, so I cleaned it out, but there was no trace of Dandelion.

"She's probably sacked out somewhere," I said. "Cats sleep a lot."

"Maybe, but where? She wasn't in the living room or anyplace else downstairs. How about your bedroom?"

"That's probably it," I said. "She was up there earlier, before I called you."

But only Hulk was on my bed, curled up and looking, as usual, like a furry beachball. She wasn't under the bed either, or down the hall in my folks' room. We even peeked into Walter's room, just in case he'd woke up and dragged her in to sleep with him, the way he tried to do now and then with Hulk.

But she wasn't there or anywhere, and Mom called a halt to our search the third time we came poking through the living room and looking under all the furniture.

"You know how cats are," she said. "They like their privacy. She's just found someplace you haven't looked yet, that's all. She'll show herself when it's time to eat in the morning."

And this time, Mom came to the door with Kathy and me, just to make sure Kathy actually got started on her way. From the way Kathy was looking at me, though, I knew she had something more to say, so I ducked out onto the front porch with her and walked her down to the sidewalk.

"I'll bet she went back to the Diefenbacher place!" Kathy said when we were out of earshot of the front door, where Mom stood watching.

"Don't be silly," I said. "Nobody's opened any doors

since you came over, and we both saw her lots of times after that."

"She let her*self* out. I don't care if she *does* get along with Hulk and your little brother and likes to get scratched behind the ears. I'll still bet she's not really a cat! And I'll bet she's out at the Diefenbacher place right now!" She sounded like she was ready to hop on her bike and check it out that very minute.

"We can go look in the morning," I said, and before I could say anything else Mom was calling me.

Back inside, Mom hustled me off to bed before I had a chance to look for Dandelion anymore, but it was quite a while before I got to sleep, and from the way she and Dad were walking around and poking their heads into my room every few minutes, I'll bet they were wondering where she'd disappeared to, too.

But she was still missing in the morning. Dad was convinced that she had slipped out when Kathy had come in. It was, after all, the only logical way she could've gotten out.

We hadn't quite finished breakfast when Kathy showed up at the door. I finished my milk and a second egg while she stood around trying not to look too impatient.

"Where are you going?" Mom asked when I started for my bicycle, chained to the front porch next to where Kathy'd parked hers.

"Just out riding," Kathy said. I didn't say anything.

"Out to the Diefenbacher place again?" Mom asked.

"We might go out past there," Kathy admitted.

For a while, I thought Mom was going to tell us to stay away from the Diefenbacher place, and, to tell the

49

truth, I'm a little surprised she didn't. Maybe I was even *hoping* she would, since I was still a little nervous after what had happened yesterday.

But she didn't. All she said was, "Be careful. And I may come out to give the place a thorough going-over myself one of these days, if Mr. Johnson doesn't show up pretty soon to sign those papers."

And we were on our way. It was sunny and already around seventy, and we'd both worked up a pretty good sweat by the time we pushed our bikes through the lane full of weeds and leaned them against the same tree we'd leaned them against yesterday. The only difference was, the ground had pretty much dried out, so our feet weren't quite as wet this time.

Dandelion wasn't in the tree, but a couple of squirrels and a half-dozen sparrows were.

I was sure it was my imagination, but even out there in the yard I had the same weird feeling I'd had the day before, the feeling that we were being watched.

"Come on," Kathy said finally, and a minute later we were pushing open the front door. She was carrying a crooked stick two or three feet long that she'd picked up in the yard.

Inside, it was the same as yesterday, only more so. Cobwebs, dust, and all that, but there weren't any cat paw prints in the dust. And our own footprints from yesterday were gone.

For a minute, Kathy just stood there in the middle of the big front room, not far from the stairs that led up to the second floor. Then, all of a sudden, she started poking the air with the stick she'd brought in.

50

"Hey!" I said, grabbing at the stick. "If they *are* here, you might hurt them, poking around that way."

She stopped poking, but she didn't put the stick down.

And that's when I definitely heard something. A door opening, from back where the kitchen was.

The door to the basement! I thought, remembering that that was one place we hadn't looked yesterday. We'd looked around the first floor, and then up on the second floor we'd gotten locked in that one room, and—

"Who's there?" Kathy asked, and I could see she was looking toward the kitchen door, too. "Whoever you are, it's okay. We know all about you, and if you're in any kind of trouble, maybe we can help. Like I told you yesterday, we helped that big hairy guy a couple weeks ago, and—"

There was a shuffling sound, or maybe a slithering one, mixed in with a sort of clicking, like a dog's toenails on a bare floor. And it sounded like it was coming through the door from the kitchen. My heart was pounding, and it was all I could do to keep from running. Kathy was peering at the empty air near the kitchen door, and I could tell she was tightening her grip on the stick she still held.

I reached out and touched her arm, and she squeaked, almost dropping the stick. "I think we better go," I said.

She looked like she was almost ready to agree, but before she could say anything there was a hissing from the kitchen, beyond whatever was making the noises.

51

A second later, Dandelion was in the doorway, her fur bushed out even more than normal. She was hissing, and underneath the hissing was a deep growl, almost as deep as Hulk's.

There were more sounds a few feet closer to us, more shuffling and toenail clicking, and then, suddenly, Dandelion, still hissing, leaped into the air toward the sounds.

Leaped, and landed.

But she didn't land on the floor.

She landed on something invisible, and she hung there, suspended, about four feet in the air, hissing.

5

"It Just Isn't Logical to Stick Something Like That in Your Pocket . . ."

For a couple of very long seconds, neither one of us did or said anything. We just watched Dandelion standing there in midair, hissing, until I finally realized that part of *her* was invisible, too.

Her feet.

All four feet had vanished, so that it didn't look so much like she was standing *on* something we couldn't see but *in* something. And one of her front legs was stretched out, like she was reaching further down into whatever she was standing in.

And then she disappeared altogether. One second she was there, the next second she wasn't. She wasn't even hissing anymore.

"I told you she was out here!" Kathy said, but she still didn't actually *do* anything. She'd even dropped the stick she'd been carrying.

A second later, Dandelion reappeared. All of her, even her feet.

At the same time, a lumpy-looking box about half the size of a rectangular Coke can also appeared, right there in midair, an inch or two from one of Dandelion's front paws.

It didn't stay suspended, however. It dropped to the floor with a dull thud.

And that's when things started getting *really* wild.

The thing whose shoulder Dandelion was standing on suddenly became visible, and it was at least as ugly as those slimy monsters they have in movies these days. It was sort of scaly-looking, and grayish green all over. And very lizardy-looking, kind of like a five-foot tyranosaur, complete with the tail but without the king-size jaws and with halfway human-looking arms and hands. It even had a face, but I can't think of what it looked like, unless maybe it was one of those stone gargoyles I saw in our geography book last year.

But what really got my attention was what was in one of its hands. It looked like a comic-book ray gun, all silvery with black streaks on it.

And it was pointed right at me.

At least it was when I first saw it. A second later, it wasn't, because the creature—lizard or whatever—was reaching down toward the lumpy box that had hit the floor a couple of seconds before.

But the box wasn't there. It had vanished again.

Then Dandelion leaped from the creature's shoulder to its head, and it let out a squeal that set my teeth on edge, sort of like somebody had scraped his fingers across a blackboard and then fed it through a rock-band amplifier. For a second, I couldn't hear anything at all, and I was even having trouble seeing, like everything had all of a sudden gotten fuzzy.

But the sound and all the rest was gone almost as quickly as they had started, and the creature was turning and running back through the kitchen, with Dandelion still clinging to its head.

As it bashed through the back door and thumped down the steps into the yard, Dandelion leaped off, landing in the weeds.

I ran to the door, where I could see the creature slogging through the weeds, heading around the trees and grapevines toward the swampy woods two or three hundred yards back. There was no sign of Dandelion, except maybe for some movement in some of the nearby weeds.

"Let's get out of here!" Kathy yelled at me suddenly. I guess even she had finally realized that hairy, ten-foot tourists who lose their spaceships are one thing, but grayish-green lizards pointing at us with things that look like guns are something else altogether.

Anyway, her yell was all it took to get me turned around and headed for the front yard and our bikes.

When we reached them, Kathy started to grab hers, but then she stopped and stuck her hand out toward me. It looked like she was holding something, but I couldn't see anything.

"Here," she said, "you take this. It won't fit in my pockets."

"Take what?"

"This! Whatever that lizard in there dropped."

And that's when I realized what she'd been doing

while I'd been looking out the back door to see what happened to Dandelion and the lizard. She'd been scrabbling around the floor looking for the invisible box.

And she'd found it.

And now she was trying to give it to me.

"Come on!" she said. "Take it! Unless you want to leave it behind!"

For a second or two, I considered it. After all, leaving it behind was the only logical thing to do. We didn't know what it was or what it could do or anything else about it. It could explode and blow us up or do almost anything, for all we knew. I mean, it just isn't logical to stick something like that in your pocket and ride off with it.

On the other hand, if we left it behind, we'd *never* find out what it was.

I held out my hand.

A second later, there was something in it. It felt hard and lumpy, like a square plastic potato. It also felt sort of wet and slimy, but it must've just been the kind of surface it had, because nothing came off on my hand.

I didn't quite drop it.

"Come on!" Kathy said again, and I noticed she was already pushing her bike through the weeds on the way to the lane and the road beyond.

For an instant, something seemed to flicker in my hand, like the thing had become visible for a half second or so and then changed its mind, but in that instant it sort of reminded me of the ring, the milorganite beeper, and it didn't seem so terrible anymore.

Which was totally illogical, but that's how it was.

So I put it in my pocket. Very carefully. I took my hanky out of that pocket so there wouldn't be anything in there but the lumpy, invisible box.

And I started pushing my bike along after Kathy's.

A couple minutes later, we were on the road, an old blacktop, and pedaling toward town.

And I had time to think. And to wonder what the thing in my pocket was.

And, worse, to wonder if the lizardy thing was going to come after us to get it back, and if that thing it had been pointing at us really *had* been a gun, and just what Dandelion really was, not to mention whether or not I was going completely crazy.

For a change, Kathy didn't say a thing. She just pedaled, and so did I. Once, I thought I heard that chalkboard screech again, way in the distance, but it turned out to be a bluejay in a tree by the side of the road. At least I think that's what it was.

About a mile down the road, still a mile or so from the highway, we slowed down. We were both getting out of breath, we'd been pedaling so hard. I sat up straight instead of crouching over the way I had been.

And I felt in my pocket, not for any logical reason but just to make sure the thing was still there and hadn't turned into something else.

All of a sudden, I felt a tingle, kind of like when the ring started beeping me, but stronger, a sort of shivery feeling all over.

I jerked my hand out of my pocket, and the bike swerved almost into the ditch before I got balanced again.

Then the tingle turned to pins and needles, also all over me.

And then I felt wet and slimy, sort of the way the box itself had felt.

And everything flickered. For two or three seconds, it was like a fluorescent light trying to get started, only it was flickers of darkness, not of light, and this was all happening out of doors, in the bright sunlight.

I grabbed for the brakes and started to yell to Kathy, but before I could make a sound, everything disappeared.

Everything disappeared—literally—and I was in total darkness, not a shred of light anywhere.

6

"What Fun Is Being Invisible if You Can't See Where You're Going?"

A *matter transmitter!* I thought, totally panicked. *That thing was a matter transmitter, and I've been sent to some other world where there isn't any sun, and I'll never get back to Earth!*

But then, maybe a half second later, I realized that I was still on my bicycle.

And the bicycle was still moving.

I could feel the wind in my face, and I could feel the little bumps in the blacktop of the road.

And then I could hear Kathy's voice, yelling, "Calvin! What in the world did you do *now?*"

Then the little blacktop bumps under the tires became the crunch of gravel and then something else, something swishy and bumpy, like tall grass at the edge of the road, and my fingers finally squeezed down on the brakes.

And the front of the bicycle dropped into something, and I went tumbling sideways. Instinctively—

something I'd picked up all those times I'd fallen off when I was learning to ride—I jumped off and twisted around on my back as I fell.

Something, probably the bike's frame, banged my shin, and I landed on my back with a thump that knocked my breath out.

I just lay there, my mind not working at all. I felt weeds and grass all around me, and I realized that the back of my shirt and pants were wet.

And I heard a bicycle falling over just a few feet away from me, and then the sound of feet running toward me.

"Calvin?"

It was Kathy's voice, of course, maybe two or three feet away.

"Calvin? What happened to you?"

And then I felt something poke at my stomach, something that felt like a finger.

"Are you okay, Calvin? *Say* something, for Pete's sake!"

"I can't *see* anything," I said, my voice kind of squeaky.

"And *I* can't see *you!* Not much of you, anyway. What did you do, turn that gadget on?"

And then, all of a sudden, I realized what had happened.

I *had* turned the gadget on, and it had made me invisible, just like that lizard thing.

And I remembered what Dad had told me that time three or four years ago when we were watching *The Invisible Man Returns* on Channel 9's *Shock-and-Schlock Theater.* If you ever really did become invisible, you'd

60

also become blind, which would sort of take the fun out of it. The thing is, the only way you could become invisible would be by becoming totally transparent, like glass or air. Which means that light would have to go right through you, without having any effect on you at all.

And if light goes right through you—right through your *eyes*—without having any effect, then you're blind. For you to be able to see, the light has to affect your eyes. The lens has to focus the light rays. The rods and cones and all that stuff in the retina have to be hit by the light rays so they can send the images to your brain.

And with the light going straight through, none of that happens, so you're blind.

I sat up, banging my head on Kathy's arm or something, and I reached into my pocket and pulled out the lumpy, invisible gadget. I poked at it, even shook it, but nothing happened.

Then I remembered what had happened back in the house. The gadget had dropped on the floor just before the lizardy thing had become visible.

I tossed it away, hearing it hit the gravel next to the blacktop of the road.

This time, nothing flickered, like it had when I'd been getting ready to vanish. Everything just reappeared, bingo, like I'd had my eyes closed and I'd just opened them.

"Calvin! You're back!"

Kathy was leaning over me. I was sitting in the ditch, the back of my clothes soaking wet from ditch goop. My bike was in the weeds three or four feet away, and

Kathy's was lying eight or ten yards down the road. Her face—well, it was as excited-looking as when she got her first real look at one of the Suits, or when we got inside that spaceship the first time.

Nervously, I looked down at myself—you know, just to make sure all of me had come back, that some bits and pieces hadn't stayed invisible.

But I was all there, right down to my right shin, which was starting to hurt from where the bike hit it while I was falling off.

"That thing you gave me," I said, "it must've been what made that miniature dinosaur invisible."

"I already knew that! How did you get it to *work?*"

"It wasn't on purpose! I just reached in my pocket for a second, and everything went black."

"But now you turned it *off* again! Where is it? What did you do to it?"

"I didn't turn it off, I threw it away."

"Threw it away? Calvin Willeford! Where—"

"Over there somewhere," I said, pointing toward the edge of the road. "I heard it hit the gravel."

She looked where I was pointing, but there was nothing there. Nothing visible, anyway. A second later, she was on her hands and knees, feeling the road.

"Come on, Calvin!" she said impatiently as she ran one hand back and forth along the surface of the black-top like a metal detector. "Help me look for it, before a car comes by and runs over it and smashes it."

And a car *was* coming!

I scrambled up out of the weeds and dropped to my knees next to Kathy, sweeping my hand back and forth, low over the blacktop, the same way she was doing.

The car was two or three hundred yards down the road when Kathy found the gadget. She didn't say anything when she found it.

But she didn't have to. She disappeared.

That is, everything but some of her hair and the baggier parts of her shirt disappeared. And the big, rolled-up cuffs on her jeans.

But it was only for a second. After a surprised-sounding squeak, she reappeared, still on her hands and knees. About the same time, the approaching car let loose a blat on its horn, and then Kathy vanished again. Again except for pieces of her clothes and a bunch of her hair, five or six inches of which just hung there in midair for a half a second and then lurched back toward the edge of the road.

And Kathy reappeared yet again, this time just as she was sitting down with a thump in the gravel off the edge of the blacktop. She was still sitting there when the car came to a stop on the other side of the road.

It was, of course, a Sheriff's Department car, with Sheriff Pippenger at the wheel. His window was rolled down and he was kind of squinting at Kathy. And scowling, but he almost always does that. Nobody's every seen him smile, so far as I know.

"Do your folks know you don't have enough brains to not play games on a public road?" he asked, spreading the frown to include me.

I started to stammer something, but Kathy—like she usually does—thought faster and came to our rescue.

"We're not playing," she said, getting on her hands and knees and acting like she was looking for something in the weeds next to the gravel berm she'd been sitting on. "We were riding by and I thought I saw a dime or something over here in the ditch and I was just looking for it."

"That's right," I agreed, but the way I sounded probably just made him more suspicious.

Anyway, he shifted his scowl all the way to me and looked for a second like he was going to get out of the car. Instead, he jerked his thumb back in the direction of the Diefenbacher place.

"I don't suppose you've been going in for a little trespassing too. Maybe even a little vandalism?"

This time neither one of us said anything. Kathy had quit poking through the weeds and was just kneeling there. Pippenger just kept scowling at us, like he was expecting us to break down and confess.

Finally, when neither of us did, he shook his head and muttered something under his breath.

"Just don't think you're getting away with anything," he said aloud. "I know all about how you kids mess around in deserted houses all around the county. And maybe some not so deserted. Just remember, I'll be keeping an eye on the whole lot of you, and so will the neighbors."

With a final scowl, he drove away. Slowly. Probably watching us in his rearview mirror. It took two or three minutes for him to disappear over the first hill less than half a mile down the road, at which point I let out a huge sigh of relief and Kathy instantly took up her search again.

64

"What happened?" she asked as she began patting the ground. "Why did I go blind when I found that thing?"

Before I could say anything, she vanished, which meant she'd found it again. But this time she was back almost instantly, and then she was making a mark in the dirt.

"So I won't lose it again," she said. "Now what's going on, anyway?"

So I told her about how invisibility really works. When I was more or less finished, she shook her head, looking irritated. "What fun is being invisible if you can't see where you're going?"

"I guess you just have to sit still," I said, shrugging. "It would be good for hiding, anyway."

"Not unless *all* of you disappears. Some of *you* was still showing, like the tips of your crewcut. And the cuffs of your jeans. What about me?"

"A lot of your hair, the part that was hanging down, not the part on top of your head. And bits and pieces of your clothes."

She shook her head. "It's probably just broken down. None of this stuff from outer space works the way it's supposed to. You can't even turn this thing off." She stopped and gave me another suspicious look. "But *you* turned it *on*. How'd you do *that?*"

"I don't have the foggiest idea. I just put my hand in my pocket, and—and nothing. A minute later, I blanked out."

"That's not much help," she said, making a face. "What we have to do is figure out how you turned it on, and then maybe we can figure out how to turn it off. If we can't, we won't even be able to pick it up without

65

disappearing." She gave me a suspicious look. "You must've pushed a button or done *something* when you stuck your hand in your pocket."

"Maybe," I said. "I remember I felt a bunch of lumps on the thing."

"But you don't know which lump you pushed?"

I shook my head. "Why don't *you* try pushing a few?"

So, after shooting me a dirty look, she did. Or I think she did. Once she picked it up, I couldn't tell *what* she was doing, since she was invisible again.

"Hey," I said after a half minute or so, "whatever you did just then made some more of your hair disappear."

All of her reappeared a couple of seconds later, leaning way over, but by then I'd noticed something else.

"Disappear again," I said.

She frowned at me but then lowered her hand to a couple of inches above the road. She vanished.

"Well?" she said a second later. "Did you figure out how to turn it off?"

"No, but I've got an idea how it works. I mean, not how it *really* works, the scientific principles or the circuits or anything like that."

"Then what *do* you mean?"

"It's a field of some kind, just like those disguise gadgets the Suits used. You know, it generates a force field or something around you, only instead of forming an image around you it just makes you invisible—transparent. And the field is the same shape you are, only a little bit bigger."

"How'd you figure that out?"

"Let me have it. I'll show you."

"It's right here," she said, pointing to a spot on the ground next to her.

She moved away a couple of feet when I came over and sat down next to it. "Just watch the ground right under me," I said, and I reached down and poked the air with my finger. Finally my finger found the gadget, and everything went black.

"There's a big dent in the ground," she said after a couple of seconds.

"That's not a dent," I said. "That's where the ground is being turned invisible. Here, I'll stand up, and you'll see a couple of foot-shaped dents. I think."

I closed my fingers around the gadget and stood up, almost. In total darkness like that, it's easy to get disoriented, maybe even dizzy. Anyway, I got halfway up and then went sprawling sideways.

"You fell over, right?" Kathy said. "Sideways, from the looks of the dent."

"Yeah," I said, releasing the gadget and reappearing. "Anyway, you see what I mean. That's why our clothes disappear, too. This thing is like an 'aura,' or a force field. Whatever's close enough to us is inside the field. That's why you could still see my cuffs. They were outside."

"Then what about our hair? That's *part* of us. Why can we still see part of *that*?"

I started to shrug, but then I remembered something from one of those science books I'd gotten from the library a couple of years ago. "The field is probably only around the part of us that's alive," I said, "like our bodies. Hair is dead."

Kathy frowned. *"Mine* isn't."

"Everybody's is," I said. "Anyway, the field only extends an inch or so beyond your body, the *live* part of your body, not including hair. Anything that sticks out beyond that can be seen."

"Disappear again," she said. "I want to try something."

I hesitated, but I disappeared. After a couple of seconds, I could hear Kathy's breathing, she was so close.

"Wow!" she said. "I guess you were right. I'm holding my finger up next to your head, and the end of it has disappeared." She made a shuddering noise. "It looks really yucky that way. You can see the inside of it, the bones and everything. It looks like the end was cut off, and—"

She broke off abruptly, and gasped, like something had just scared her half to death.

7

"Interstellar Sneezing Powder?"

"**W**hat happened?" I asked, dropping the gadget and reappearing. Kathy had jumped back from me.

"I—I don't know! It was like I'd picked that thing up again! Only I didn't!"

"You disappeared?"

"I guess so. I mean, everything went black for just a second."

"Maybe the field expanded or something," I said.

Kathy backed away another couple of feet. "You think so?"

"I don't know. You said you were poking the end of your finger into the aura, didn't you? Maybe that—" All of a sudden I had an idea. "Did you maybe actually touch me?" I asked.

"Maybe. Why?"

"Come on, let's find that thing again. It's on the ground here somewhere."

We waited while a car whizzed by—not Pippenger's—and then it took us another couple of minutes of feeling the road, but we did find it again. This time it was in the weeds that bordered the ditch. It must've bounced when I dropped it.

"Here it is," I said, reappearing after another momentary disappearance when I first touched it. "This time, pick it up with just one hand, and I'll hang on to your other hand."

She frowned at me for a second, but she took my hand anyway. Then she reached down and groped around in the weeds and closed her fingers around something.

Everything went black, just like when I had picked it up myself.

I let go of Kathy's hand.

Everything reappeared. Except Kathy, of course.

"Is your hand still where it was?" I asked.

"I think so. Why?"

I groped around in the air a little more, and touched her hand again.

And went blind again.

"What do you think you're doing, Calvin Willeford?" Kathy asked sternly after a couple more disappearances and reappearances. "I'm going to put this thing down, right now!"

"Okay," I said. "I've got it figured out, more or less."

"So tell me about it," she said, reappearing as she bent over and put the gadget on the ground. This time she made a little mark in the gravel next to where she had put it.

"Whatever the field is," I said, "it must be contagious or something like that. As long as you're holding that thing, anybody that touches you disappears, too. That's what must've happened before, while *I* was invisible. You were poking your finger around inside the field, and you accidentally touched me, and *you* disappeared. That's all."

Kathy shivered. "That's spooky," she said. "Now how about figuring out how to turn it off?"

"Maybe you should try," I said. "You already figured out how to make the field bigger. Maybe you could just do the same thing, only backwards, and it would—"

"*I* don't know what I did!"

"You must have *some* idea! Which bumps were you squeezing? Which way were you holding it?"

"Which bumps did *you* squeeze when you turned it on in the first place? Nobody was disappearing at all until you started poking around with it in your pocket."

"I wasn't poking at it when I disappeared," I said, trying to remember just when I *had* disappeared. "I just reached in my pocket and touched it, and I started feeling tingly, and I jerked my hand out, and that was when it happened."

Kathy frowned. "But if you weren't touching it, how come you disappeared?"

"I don't know," I started to say, but then I put my hand in my pocket again. And I knew what had happened.

"There's a hole," I said. "That thing must've been touching my leg through the hole in my pocket."

"But you *had* been poking at it. We both had it in our

71

hands back at the Diefenbacher place, but we didn't disappear *then*. Something you did must've turned it on."

"Maybe," I said. "Or maybe it came back on by itself."

Which, now that I thought about it, made sense. That first time, I hadn't just disappeared instantly, the way we did later each time we touched the thing. Instead, everything had flickered, like a fluorescent light getting started.

Or like something with a loose wire that's just been shaken back into place so that it's starting to make a connection again.

I told Kathy, and she just hmphed. "You're probably right," she said. "It must be another one of their bargain-basement gadgets. I bet their high-priced models let you see where you're going." She paused and glared at the spot where she'd laid it down. "But how are we going to get the thing home if we can't turn it off?"

"No problem," I said, realizing instantly I shouldn't have said anything until I found out if the idea I'd just had would really work.

Leaning down, I picked the gadget up. Everything went black, of course, but a second later, when I put it in my pocket—the other pocket, the one without the hole—everything went back to normal.

"It's okay as long as we don't actually touch it," I said, and then, to be on the safe side, I wrapped a handkerchief around it, managing to vanish only twice while I was doing it.

The rest of the way back to town, neither one of us said a word. I don't know why Kathy was so quiet, but as for me, I didn't say much mainly because the only thing I could think of to say was, "Maybe we should take this back and leave it where we found it," and I knew what kind of a hit that would make with her. Maybe I was even thinking about taking it back myself, without telling her. In fact, I *know* I thought about it. I'm just not one hundred percent sure I *meant* it. I mean, if I had really meant it, I would've gone ahead and done it. Right? But I didn't.

As for Kathy, she had convinced herself that my Uncle Harold had the answers to the tourists and the invisibility gadgets and everything, and she spent as much time as she could that day pumping Mom and Dad about him. She didn't find out a lot more than I'd already told her, though. The planet the visitors had supposedly come from was "Thuseria," not "Wisteria" like I'd said, and it had even made the papers in Carrollton, where he'd lived then. The "Message" that had never shown up was supposed to be the "secret of living in harmony with the Universe and with each other." Apparently Uncle Harold and a reporter from the Carrollton paper had sat up all one night waiting with a wire recorder and a flash camera, but nothing was seen or heard. And a week later, Uncle Harold said it had all been his imagination, maybe helped along by an extra beer before going to bed on the night he'd first seen the Thuserians.

And he never talked about them again.

"And I would appreciate it," Dad said, giving Kathy a stern look, "if you would refrain from pestering him about it when we go out there tomorrow. And that goes for all of you," he added, giving me and Mom the

73

same look. Mom just shrugged, like she didn't feel like arguing about it. I got the feeling, though, that she might've talked to Uncle Harold about it a little more than she'd told Dad.

"Can we tell him about the monster some of the kids saw at school last week?" Kathy asked.

"I don't think that would be wise," Dad said. "He might think you were making fun of him."

Kathy sighed. "Okay," she said, but I knew from the way she looked that she was hatching some kind of plan.

To tell the truth, I was having second thoughts about Uncle Harold's visitors myself. Maybe they *had* been real. Sure, they were impossible-sounding, but not much more so than the ones Kathy and I'd run into.

For that matter, Kathy's idea that they might've been missionaries sort of made sense. I mean, there's all kinds of missionaries, including some pretty weird ones, and that business about "living in harmony with the universe" sounded like the sort of thing some of the far-out ones would say.

Or maybe, instead of missionaries, they'd all been practical jokers trying to play a trick on the "primitive earthling." I'd read a couple science fiction stories like that, where people from outer space came to Earth just to play jokes on us.

Maybe this whole thing—Uncle Harold's visitors, our "tourists," the lizards, the invisibility gadget—was just one big practical joke.

Interstellar sneezing powder?

But why would they pick Uncle Harold—or *us*—to play jokes on? It didn't make sense. Besides, that tourist we'd saved had sure *seemed* sincere, not to mention almost dead there at the last. But who knows what sort of a sense of humor people from outer space have?

Anyway, I did a lot of thinking that evening, although maybe "thinking" isn't the right word. Dithering might be more like it. The trouble was, logical thinking didn't really help. One idea was just as crazy as the next, so all I could do was let my mind hop around from one to the other and try to keep from falling in the cracks, of which there were plenty. I was also hoping that, despite Dad's warnings, Kathy and I would have a chance to talk to Uncle Harold. Alone.

If we did, *maybe* he'd be able to tell us something that made sense.

But a little after two o'clock that night, I just about gave up the idea that the lizards were either superscientific practical jokers or outer-space missionaries. It started when I woke up and found Walter standing next to my bed, poking at my shoulder.

"I'm scared, Calvin," he said, and his voice was kind of trembling, just like it had been when he'd gotten close to one of the Suits, one of the aliens.

8

"The Lizards Have Come to Get Me!"

A second later, while I was still trying to think of something to say, there was a crashing noise from somewhere downstairs, like a chair or something had been knocked over.

And then a yowl, like whatever had been knocked over had landed on Hulk's tail.

The lizards have come to get me! I thought, totally panicked, trying to remember where I'd put the invisibility gadget and wondering whether if I found it and threw it down the stairs to them, they'd go away and leave me alone.

I tried to get out of bed, but Walter was pressed up against the edge, pinning the sheets down. By the time I got Walter to back up a couple of inches so I could get out—the other side of my bed's against the wall—the hall light had come on, and I heard Dad at the head of the stairs.

"All right!" he was shouting in his best "Bad cat!" voice. "What's going on down there?"

Then he was coming down the hall, and a second later he looked in my room. He blinked when he saw Walter, then frowned. "Walter, go back to bed. It's just Hulk."

"Not Hulk!" Walter said emphatically.

But Dad wasn't paying any attention. He took Walter by the hand and headed across the hall to Walter's room. "And you," he said over his shoulder at me, "go see what your monster smashed this time."

"But Dad—"

"Now!" he said.

I had finally remembered where I'd put the invisibility gadget—under the mattress, now wrapped not in a handkerchief but a pillow case—but before I could get to it, there was another crash downstairs and Dad was back, practically dragging me out into the hall.

Then there was a different sound.

The sound of the screen door slamming shut.

Dad stopped, teetering with one foot on the top stair step.

"Cats don't open doors," he muttered and started to back up. "Not even Hulk."

Pulling me with him, he had us inside his and Mom's bedroom in a couple of seconds. "Call the sheriff," he said to Mom in a loud whisper, and then he grabbed Walter, who had already come back into the hall from his own room, and pulled him into the bedroom with the rest of us.

By the time he had the bedroom door locked, Mom had gotten the sheriff's office on the phone.

"We're supposed to stay where we are," she said when she hung up a minute later. "Don't try to confront them."

"I have no intention of confronting *anyone!*" Dad said, looking at the locked door to the hall. Mom had an arm around Walter, who was looking calmer now.

As for me, I was listening for lizardy footsteps in the hall and hoping it was just the invisibility gadget they were after, not me.

But there weren't any footsteps, lizardy or otherwise. In fact, there wasn't a single sound. There hadn't been any since the door had slammed.

Then, after four or five minutes, we could see the flashes of a squad car as it pulled up in front of the house. We waited until we heard the front door open downstairs and a voice calling Mom's name.

"We're up here," Dad said, opening the door to the hall.

"This is Deputy Crandal, sir," the voice called back. "It looks as if it's all clear down here."

"I thought it might be," Dad said as we all started down the stairs. "I heard the screen door slam just before we called you."

The deputy, standing in the middle of the front room, nodded as he looked around. A bookcase not far from the door, a small one with glass doors, was knocked over, one of the doors broken. A floor lamp that had stood next to it was also flattened, its shade knocked cockeyed.

"Must've heard you moving around and then ran," the deputy said. "Most burglars will do that. Although this looks more like vandalism than burglary."

"Where's Hulk?" I asked.

"Hulk?" The deputy looked at me.

"My cat. A big—"

"There was a small tiger on the porch, if that's what you mean."

I pulled loose from Dad and ran to the porch. Hulk was on the railing, his tail bushed way out. And he was growling, down deep in his throat, sounding almost like a dog.

"Careful," Dad called. "He can be pretty unpredictable when he's upset."

"It's okay," I said, but I took it easy, reaching out cautiously to touch his back.

He jerked around, hissing at the touch, almost falling off the railing. (At twenty pounds, he's very active, but a little clumsy now and then.) His almost-accident, though, seemed to calm him down, like maybe it made him remember where he was or something.

Anyway, he wasn't growling or hissing anymore, and after a few seconds he hopped down off the railing with his usual thump. To make sure he didn't wander off the porch, I picked him up and lugged him into the house.

That was when I noticed that his paws were wet, and there were a couple of wet spots on his chest. My first thought was that he'd gotten hurt, maybe gotten cut when the bookcase shattered, and I set him down on the floor to get a better look.

A second later, when I looked at the wet stuff that had come off on my hands, I realized that Hulk was all right. I also realized it was a good thing that Mom and Dad and Deputy Crandal were busy looking at the stuff that had been knocked over, not at me or my hands.

The wet stuff did look sort of like blood, but it sure wasn't Hulk's. Not *my* Hulk's, anyway.

It was green and—although this last may've just been my imagination—very lizardy-looking.

Needless to say, I didn't get much sleep the rest of the night. Just a plain old burglary would've been enough to make me nervous, but this had been a burglary where the burglar left green blood behind and had probably been trying to reclaim what Kathy and I had burglarized from *him* in the first place.

Actually, after Deputy Crandal left and we got the glass from the bookcase door picked up and we all got back to bed, I was seriously considering digging the gadget out from under my mattress and pedaling it out to the Diefenbacher place even if it *was* still an hour or two till the sun came up. I also thought about just heaving it out the window or dumping it in a neighbor's trashcan.

But somehow I never got around to any of it.

For one thing, I remembered that the lizardy-looking thing had been pointing at me with that thing that looked like a gun *before* we found his invisibility gadget. Maybe, I thought, it was only *because* we had taken it away from him that he hadn't been able to finish us off yet.

For that matter, maybe it was the ring that had caused the trouble. Maybe the lizardy-looking aliens were hereditary enemies of the hairy ones, and maybe he'd seen the ring and figured I was on the hairy guy's side and therefore I was an enemy, too, and had to be wiped out. Maybe I should throw the *ring* away, not the invisibility gadget. I mean, I knew the ring could pick up signals the tourists put out, so why couldn't it be putting out a signal of its own, a signal that the lizards could home in on, even when they were invisible and couldn't see anything?

But you get the idea. If you don't know the rules or even who the players are, it's kind of hard to do what's logical. You try to figure out what's going on and what you should do about it, but you just keep thinking of different ways of looking at things and you end up going around not just in circles but in curlicues.

Finally, I "decided" that Kathy's hunch about talking to Uncle Harold might be our best bet after all. Her hunches had been pretty good so far. Besides, UFO people from Thuseria with a message for humanity was sounding saner all the time. I mean, it wasn't really that much crazier than what we'd already run into.

None of this, however, helped me get any sleep, and in the morning, for the first time ever, I was really anxious to get started for Uncle Harold's. Apparently Kathy was, too. She showed up at our place at least an hour before Mom had told her we'd pick her up, and by the time I'd told her about the "burglary" she was practically hopping up and down.

"Where's the whatchamacallit?" she asked. "You *are* taking it along, aren't you?"

"It's in my pocket," I said.

I'd put it in a Baggie, figuring that would be safer than wrapping it in a handkerchief. I mean, I'd hate to disappear while we were on the road. Having someone sitting next to you vanish right out from under his safety belt could be sort of distracting, even to Dad, and distracting someone while he's driving isn't the brightest thing you could do.

"And nobody knows about it yet?" Kathy asked.

I shook my head. "But maybe we *should* tell someone. Mom, maybe. *She* ought to believe us."

"Anybody'd *believe* us. All we have to do is vanish right in front of their eyes. But then they'd take it away from us, and who knows what else they'd do? Remember what Sheriff Pippenger tried to do to that guy we helped out. If it hadn't been for us, Pippenger would've killed him for sure. If he ever finds out about this invisibility watchamacallit, and he finds out where we got it, he'd probably want to drop a *bomb* on the Diefenbacher place. Besides, why do you want to tell anyone about it, anyway?"

I didn't have a good answer, and even if I had had one Kathy would've topped it one way or the other.

We got to Uncle Harold's place, a farmhouse without a farm but with an orchard and a bunch of abandoned outbuildings, a little before noon. Uncle Harold's in his seventies, I guess, and really skinny. Sort of like me, only taller and older and without much hair. Other times I'd brought something along to read, or went walking through some nearby woods, since he and Mom and Dad usually did most of the talking, which normally wasn't that much anyway, except when Dad had some new project at work that he was enthused about.

This time, however, I could tell that things were going to be different right from the start, and not just because Kathy and I wanted a chance to grill him about forty years ago. We'd only been there a few minutes when Uncle Harold asked about the "monster" that had been spotted at our school.

Dad frowned at Kathy and me and asked Uncle Harold how he had heard about it.

"It made the papers all the way down here," he said with a grin. "One of those 'silly season' stories, I guess. Said something about your Sheriff Pippenger makin' a fool of himself tryin' to arrest an imitation rock, too."

"I don't like to speak ill of the law," Dad said, "but personally I suspect the man had been drinking on duty, that's all."

"Maybe so, but the papers said a bunch of kids had seen something pretty weird, too, right there in the schoolyard. I don't suppose you two saw anything?" he asked, looking at Kathy and me. "Firsthand, I mean, with your own eyes?"

We both shrugged, not very convincingly, I guess. About the same time, Dad shook his head and explained how we "hadn't really seen much of anything, just someone in an ape suit," which was more or less what Kathy and I had both told our folks at the time.

As for Uncle Harold, he just looked at us for a second or two and then seemed to tune us out the way he does sometimes. But then, after only another five or ten minutes, he got up from the kitchen table where we'd all been sitting, talking mostly about the weather.

"I just remembered," he said, looking at Mom and Dad. "I was lookin' through that trunk of Grace's stuff in the attic the other day, you know the one." Grace was Aunt Grace, Uncle Harold's wife. She'd died five or six years ago, about the time I was starting to school. "It seems a shame for it to all go to waste up there, just gatherin' dust. Why don't you two take a look through it, maybe you'd find something you've got a use for." He paused, glancing sideways at Walter. "And I know how Walt likes to fool around up there. Never know what you'll find, eh, kiddo?"

He winked at Walter, who was already on his feet, grinning. If there was one thing Walter liked more than scratching Hulk behind the ears, it was exploring attics or old houses or almost anything like that. Last year, when he was six, I'd given him a ride on the bike out to one of those other abandoned houses—not the Diefenbacher place, but another one closer to town—and he'd had the time of his life, even if all he ever found was a lot of dust and couple of old rusty rat traps.

Dad hesitated, looking suspiciously at me and Kathy, but Mom was on her feet right away. "That sounds like a very good idea," she said, and I'd swear there was an almost-wink between her and Uncle Harold. Or maybe she just wanted to look through the stuff in the attic, too, like Walter. I mean, she did once say one of the reasons she started selling real estate was the chance it gave her to look through a lot of strange houses, so maybe exploring like that runs in the family.

"And you, young man," Uncle Harold said, looking at me, "why don't you and I go outside and stretch our legs a little. You always look like you could use some exercise, work up an appetite so you'll put a little meat on your bones. You too, young lady, although you look like you're in better shape than that beanpole nephew of mine."

And then we were outside, following the path back toward the barn and the other outbuildings. Beyond them and to one side were the woods I'd wandered around in on other trips. I don't know who owns them, but the one time I met anyone, it was somebody about Dad's age, and he just waved, didn't order me off or anything like that.

"Well," Uncle Harold said when we were thirty or forty yards from the house, down between the remains of a barn and what I guess had been a chicken house at one time. Back here, except for the path, it looked almost like the Diefenbacher place, all overgrown and everything. The house and yard—the only part Uncle Harold actually owns, Dad had said once—were kept in good shape, but whoever owned the rest of it hadn't done anything for years. The woods and the pasture on the other side—where I'd seen some cows a couple of times, and once some horses—were in better shape.

"Well," Uncle Harold repeated after a few seconds. "From the way you two looked when I asked if you'd seen that 'monster,' I'll bet there's a little something you ain't told your folks. Or anybody else, for that matter. Am I right?"

"What about the things *you* saw?" Kathy asked abruptly.

"Me? Who said *I* saw anything?"

"You know, back forty or fifty years ago. The flying saucer or whatever it was."

"You know about that, huh?"

"Mom told us," I said, "but Dad didn't want us to mention it to you. He said it might embarrass you."

He looked at the two of us, kind of grinning. "Depends," he said, "on what *you* two saw."

"Then you *did* see something!" Kathy said, her excitement breaking out all over her again. "I *knew* it! But why did you—"

"Whoa! Hold on a second there! You first. Cal?"

So we told him. Most of it, anyway. As we wandered on past the barn and along a path through the orchard, we told him about how I got the ring and how both of us saved the stranded tourist from Sheriff Pippenger.

But that was as far as we got, at least right then. We were just getting ready to start on the invisible lizards when a soft, silky, not-quite-squeaky voice came from somewhere down in the grass.

"I rather thought you might be the 'Uncle Harold' these two were talking about," it said.

A second later, Dandelion emerged onto the path only inches from Uncle Harold's feet.

9

"A Good Number of Your Species Really *Are* Fruitcakes."

"If these two were doin' the talkin', I must be," Uncle Harold said, and he didn't bat an eye over the fact that it was a cat that he was answering. He just looked down at her. "What are *you* doin' back in town, and how'd you come to meet my nephew and his friend? That big hairy thing they were talkin' about sure didn't sound like you."

"It wasn't," the same high-pitched but somehow silky voice said. "I just met them a couple of days ago. *I* saved *their* hides, as a matter of fact."

"You *are* from outer space!" Kathy said, her voice almost as high as Dandelion's. "I knew it! I just knew it!"

"Saved their hides?" Uncle Harold broke in, his voice suddenly serious. "What were they doing that their hides required saving?"

"It's a long story, Hal."

Hal? Uncle Harold was "Hal"?

I don't know why, but that one word jumped out and sidetracked me totally for a few seconds. I mean, it really twisted my mind around more than any of this other stuff, like Dandelion being an alien and all that. See, whenever I'd thought about Uncle Harold and his UFO encounter, I'd always pictured him looking pretty much the same way he does now, which I guess was just plain dumb. I mean, I *knew* it had all happened forty or fifty years ago, and I'd seen his wedding picture with Aunt Grace dozens of times on the wall in his living room, but that was just a picture.

Or it had been until that second, when Dandelion called him "Hal." Now, all of a sudden, I knew—really *knew*—that the person in that picture had been real, and that that's what Uncle Harold had really looked like at one time. That's what he'd looked like when he'd seen his UFO. When he'd been called Hal.

Weird, really weird, the way one little thing, just a name, can have an effect like that on you. Or on me, anyway. Maybe it's just me that's weird.

Anyway, when I came out of my little trance, Uncle Harold was frowning. "I've got plenty of time," he was saying.

"Let's just say your nephew and his friend were in the wrong place at the wrong time," Dandelion said, "and saying the wrong things to the wrong people."

"The wrong people? That makes it sound like you're here on business again."

Her fur riffled slightly, almost as if she were shrugging somewhere inside it all. "Why else? This isn't the garden spot of the galaxy, you know. Which reminds me, Hal, did you ever give up that absolutely deadly little habit you used to have?"

"You mean the cigarettes?" he asked, his frown turning to a faint grin as he shook his head. "After what you told me, I gave them up cold turkey. Haven't touched a one since. But you were going to tell me what Calvin and his friend here were doing that you had to 'save their hides,' as you put it."

"I was?"

"You were," he said, the frown threatening to return. "After bringing it up, you at least owe me an explanation."

There was another riffle of her fur, followed by a whispered sigh. "Very well," she said. "I suppose you're right. But as I said, it's a long story."

"Like *I* said, we've got plenty of time," he said. "And since these young folks here don't know what happened last time, maybe you should fill them in on that too."

She cocked her head on one side as she looked up at him. "You know, Hal, for a rather primitive anthropoid, you can be very pushy at times."

"Good thing, too, at least as far as you're concerned."

There was another whispered sigh, almost a purr, and then she hopped—floated?—to a head-high branch of an apple tree a few feet away.

"Very well," she said, looking down at us as she curled her tail around herself in the royal-cushion fashion she'd used before, "what do you wish to know?"

"For a start," Kathy, unable to contain herself any longer, burst out, "what do you *really* look like?"

89

The cat's yellow eyes gave Kathy the kind of look Hulk gives me on those rare occasions when I manage to find some kind of food he doesn't like. "I believe you people have a saying. What you see is what you get."

"That isn't a disguise, then? That's what you really look like?"

"Of course. Do you not find it attractive?"

"Better say yes," Uncle Harold put in. "She can get a little touchy."

"But if this is what you really look like," Kathy persisted, "how do you *do* anything? You don't even have any claws, let alone hands. That big hairy thing had *hands*, at least."

Dandelion continued to stare at Kathy for several seconds, but then she daintily held up one of her front paws. As we watched, a set of tiny fingers popped into view. It was pretty much like any other cat's retractable claws, only these apparently were retractable fingers. Fully retractable.

"Do these meet with your approval?" she asked.

And that's the way it went for the next half hour or so. If I cut out the sarcasm and all the rest (on both sides) what it all amounted to was, Dandelion was an agent—a "top agent," she *said*—for some law enforcement agency or other, one that had jurisdiction just about everywhere in the galaxy. A sort of feline Lensman, I guess, except that she probably didn't go in for blasters and world wrecking and all that stuff that the original Lensman did in all those space operas I read last year.

She didn't object to the name Dandelion, either, which made me wonder if I'd thought of it all by myself or if I'd had a little nudge from one of her gadgets, one she wasn't telling us about.

Anyway, she'd first come to Earth forty-some years ago. She was on the trail of what she called "renegades who were interfering with the orderly and natural development of human civilization," which got a sarcastic snort from Kathy. Dandelion just gave her another look and added quietly, "You should see *some* of the worlds I've worked on. Yours isn't that bad, all things considered." She wouldn't, however, say just what it was these villains had been up to.

"But what about Thuseria?" I asked at one point. "And that message you were going to give everybody? I mean, what's that got to do with being an agent or whatever?"

"That's just their way of keeping things secret," Uncle Harold put in when Dandelion didn't say anything for a few seconds. "See, it's like this. First time I saw her, she *was* wearing some kind of disguise, like those tourists you were tellin' me about."

"Hardly like *them!*" Dandelion put in. "Their equipment is the pits, for one thing! And I am not the least surprised that one of them lost his ship. From your description, he—it—was a Daschkor, from the planet of the same name, a planet *not* widely known for the intelligence or ingenuity of its inhabitants."

"Thuseria," I reminded them.

"Oh, yes," Uncle Harold said, "Thuseria. See, like I started to say, first time I saw her, she looked more or less human but about seven feet tall, wearing some kind of Oriental-looking outfit and floating a foot off the ground. And glowing. And she told me this wild story

91

about the planet she was from and how they'd figured out how wars and disease were all caused by 'bad cosmic vibrations,' and that they were goin' to tell us humans how to live in harmony and get rid of all the bad vibrations so we could be perfect, just like they were on Thuseria. Thing is, I wasn't supposed to tell anyone. I'd been 'chosen' to be the first to learn all this stuff, what you'd call a pilot project, I guess. But it was supposed to be our little secret until the rest of the Thuserians got here. That was when they were goin' to tell everyone else."

"But that doesn't make any sense," I said. "If she was really here to help Earth, why would she—"

"Just hold your horses, Calvin. That's what I'm tryin' to tell you. Now, like I said, I wasn't supposed to tell anyone. Thing is, I ain't worth a plugged nickel at keepin' things a secret. I knew it didn't really make any sense, but I *believed* her. I mean, wouldn't *you* believe someone who could glow in the dark and float a foot off the ground? Anyway, I just couldn't sit on somethin' like that, so I told a buddy of mine about it, a guy that worked on the paper, and the next thing I knew—well, she came back, still floatin' and glowin', and told me another shipful would be showin' up in a few days. And she told me right where it would be, so my buddy and I were right there, waitin' with a camera and a recorder."

He paused and glanced at Dandelion, who just riffled her fur again.

"Of course nothin' happened," he went on. "I just sat there in the woods like a blame fool, and my buddy got mad and wouldn't talk to me anymore, and then he wrote the whole thing up in the paper, makin' me look like a fool all over the state."

"I *told* you not to tell anyone, Hal," Dandelion said, and she sounded like she was smirking just a little.

"Sure, but tellin's just what you wanted me to do. Or *expected* me to do, anyway." He looked back at Kathy and me. "See, after that was all over, she came back, lookin' like herself this time, and she told me the truth. I think. Same story she's tellin' you now, anyway. See, the thing is, those people she works for don't want hardly anyone to know she's here, but she wanted somebody's help. And if she just came straight out and told the truth the first time and then asked the guy to help, and then he shot off his mouth—well, there's a little bit of a chance somebody might believe him. Not much of a chance, but a chance. This way, though— who's gonna believe some nut who's already proved what a fruitcake he is?"

Kathy let out a low whistle. "Wow!" she said. "So *that's* where all those really far-out stories in the UFO magazines come from! It's just you outer-space agents covering yourselves!"

"A few of them," Dandelion admitted. "But a good number of your species, I'm afraid, really *are* fruitcakes."

"But what did you want Uncle Harold for?" I asked. "I mean, as far advanced as you are, what could—"

"Let us just say that, no matter how primitive the planet, it is always good to have someone to turn to in the event of an emergency. And there is the matter of being understaffed," she added, and now she was sounding a bit annoyed. "Can you believe that I alone am responsible for this entire sector? For nearly one hundred inhabited planets spread throughout more than ten thousand cubic parsecs? I am, as you would say, spread very thin."

"She wanted me to keep an eye out," Uncle Harold said, "just in case some pals of that bunch she'd already gotten rid of showed up again. She couldn't stick around herself, not forever, so she gave me one of these."

At which point he pulled out his pocket watch, an old gold-plated model, the same one I'd seen him using on other visits.

"What's *that*?" Kathy asked, glancing back and forth between it and my ring. "Is that another beeper? Something that lets her give you a call whenever she's in the neighborhood?"

"No, this lets *me* call *her*." He poked at the stem for a second, and Dandelion's collar took on a blue glow. "Like that."

One of her paws flicked at the collar, and the glow faded. "I would appreciate it if you did not generate any more false alarms, Hal," she said, "at least not in such close quarters, thank you."

"Sorry," he said with a quick grin.

"So you were a lookout?" Kathy asked. "But how could you tell if one of these guys came around? I mean, if they could disguise themselves any old way—"

Uncle Harold held up the watch again. "This thing lets me know. See, whenever one of those disguise makers or any of their other gadgets are operating anywhere in the neighborhood, this lets me know." He glanced at Dandelion. "Or I guess what it really does is, it uses me—or whoever's got hold of it—kind of like an antenna. But however it does it, it makes it so I can feel whatever it is those other gizmos put out. Not *her* gizmo, of course, since all she wanted me to watch for were those other guys, not her. Anyway, whenever I felt anything, I was supposed to give her a call." He started to poke at the stem again, but he quit after a sidelong glance at Dandelion.

"Makes *you* feel it!" Kathy said, looking excited again. "Has that little brother of Calvin's ever played with that watch?"

"He did get his hands on it once," Uncle Harold said. "Why?"

"From what Calvin says, Walter gets jumpy whenever one of these aliens comes around. The ones that disguise themselves, anyway. Maybe he got himself turned on when he was fooling around with the watch, but he never got turned off."

"That is quite impossible," Dandelion said. "The device enhances the operator's nervous system only temporarily and returns it to normal the instant contact is broken."

"Maybe it's *supposed* to be returned to normal," Kathy said, "but none of those gadgets of yours that we've seen so far ever seem to work quite the way they're supposed to."

Dandelion gave Kathy a disbelieving look, sort of like what I get from Hulk if I push him out of his favorite chair so I can sit down. "If you are speaking of what those overgrown lummoxes from Daschkor carry around with them, you are quite right. However, there is no comparison between their equipment and mine, I assure you."

Kathy didn't look convinced, but for a change, she didn't push it. Instead, she said, "As long as we're talking about alien detectors, what about that cat of Calvin's? He didn't look like he was bothered by you."

"And why should he be? His senses are even easier to fool than are yours."

"You mean you *are* disguised?" Kathy said.

"Not visually, which I assumed is what you were inquiring about previously. For other species, there are other disguises. Your pet's species, for example, depends largely on a sense of smell, so a slight alteration in that area is all that is required. As I said, my equipment is quite a different matter from that of the Daschkor. Even when theirs is working properly—which, as you have noted, is not all that often—they work only on visual and tactile levels. Their odors are masked to some extent, but not enough to fool any species with a highly developed sense of smell."

"Speaking of equipment not working right," Kathy said, "that ring of Calvin's was acting up the night you were at his place. It was just like when one of those tourists gave him a call, only it didn't tell him where to go. I don't suppose you know what was going on?"

"Merely a test," Dandelion said. "I wanted to be positive that it was indeed a standard, if technologically inferior, milorganite device."

"You didn't believe us?" Kathy asked, frowning.

"What about that invisible lizard you jumped on?" I asked, trying to get the conversation back to something more practical. "Who is he? And is he one of the bad guys you're after this time?"

"Most assuredly," she said, turning toward Uncle Harold. "I hope you're paying attention, Hal. This is the answer to your original question. You remember, the one about why their hides need saving?"

He nodded. "I figured you'd get around to it sooner or later."

"It would have been sooner had you not insisted on such elaborate background information. However, that is neither here nor there," she said, turning back to Kathy and me.

"You two are very fortunate," she went on, "very fortunate indeed. Had I not been present when you barged in, mistakenly proclaiming to know all about that creature, I am reasonably certain he would have used his weapon on you. Of one thing you may be certain—he and his associates want no one to know of even their existence, let alone their purpose."

"What *is* their purpose?" Kathy asked.

"There is no need to concern yourself with that."

"And that thing that made him invisible—how does it work?"

"Have you not been able to unravel its workings for yourself? You have had it for more than two days." She was being sarcastic again—I think.

"We figured out it makes whoever's touching it transparent to light," I said. "That's why you can't see anything when it makes you invisible."

"You have used it, then?"

I nodded and tried to explain what had happened on the way back from the Diefenbacher place. Dandelion's yellow eyes looked from Kathy to me and back as we started to talk, and after the first few sentences she gave Uncle Harold one of her fur-riffling looks. He didn't say anything, but I could tell he was paying extra-close attention to us now.

"Once again you have been fortunate," she said, cutting us off before we had finished. "The device you have been playing with is little better than a toy, but it can be dangerous in inexperienced hands such as yours. And there is always the possibility that one of those creatures would track you down and try to take it from you."

"One of them already did," I said and raced through what had happened last night, including the green blood on Hulk's claws. Needless to say, Uncle Harold didn't miss a word, and from his expression it was hard to tell how he was taking it.

"Interesting," Dandelion said when we finished. "Once more you appear to have had more good fortune than you deserve. Your pet's superficial resemblance to my own species is in all likelihood the major reason the creature was routed so easily. However, you cannot count on such luck to save you a second time. It would be best if you relinquished the device to me and—"

All of a sudden, Dandelion stopped talking, and her ears stiffened the way Hulk's do when he sees a bird on the other side of a windowpane.

And her collar began to glow.

Not the bright-blue glow like when Uncle Harold had "called" her, but a fainter, pinkish glow.

Her paws—her hands, actually, since the tiny retractable fingers had already sprung out—darted to her collar. In the same instant, she leaped from the tree branch, straight toward the three of us.

For a split second, it looked like she'd turned into a pink, glowing version of those flying squirrels you see in nature films, where they jump from the top of a tree and spread all four legs out, and the flaps of fur unfold like a glider, and away they go like a fur-covered paper airplane.

But like I said, that was only for a split second.

In the *next* split second, she was just a big glow in midair, like one of those little balls of light that zipped around in *Close Encounters*.

And then she was a *big* glow.

Then the glow was all around us. That was all we could see, anywhere, just a big glow. It had swallowed us up. We were inside it. We couldn't see anything else, not even each other.

The only logical thing to do was panic, but, for the life of me, this time I couldn't think how to do it.

10

"What Was *That* All About?"

I'm not sure how long it took for the glow to settle down and become something else, but it seemed like forever.

The first thing I saw when it did was Kathy. She was a couple feet to my left, just like she had been before. Her mouth was wide open, but she wasn't saying anything.

She was just glowing.

Next I saw Uncle Harold. He looked pretty calm, considering the fact that he was glowing even brighter than Kathy.

Then I looked down and saw myself.

I was glowing, too. Me, my clothes, everything.

Radioactivity! I thought suddenly. *We're all radioactive!*

But that idea was too silly to last more than a second or two. If you ever got radioactive enough to glow, you'd also be several times radioactive enough to be dead and boiled.

Besides, the glow had started to fade by then, and I could see that we were all inside a room of some sort.

A small, yellow room. A small, yellow room with soft, furry walls. And a soft, furry floor, even a soft, furry ceiling. At least they all *looked* soft, and I could *feel* how soft the floor was under my feet, sort of like the thickest, plushest rug you could imagine.

It took another five or ten seconds to spot Dandelion, since she was practically the same color as the room. She was hovering in midair, floating upright a few inches off the floor, her tail curled around her yogi-folded back legs. In the wall in front of her was a screen, maybe three inches across, and below the screen was a keyboard, covered with thirty or forty keys even smaller than the keys they have on those credit-card-size pocket calculators. But they were just the right size for Dandelion's retractable fingers, and she was tapping away like a high-speed typist. Almost invisible symbols—light yellow on a dark-yellow background—streaked across the tiny screen.

"What happened?" Kathy was the first one to get her voice back, but it sounded muffled, as if the furry, cushioned walls soaked up the sound.

"We're inside Dandelion's ship," Uncle Harold said.

"Inside her ship? But where'd it come from?"

"She carries it around with her. You saw it, right there around her neck."

"Her *collar* is a *spaceship?*" That was me, not Kathy. Kathy was looking around, starting to get that expression that usually means she's figured out how something or other works.

"Why not?" she said, her expression completing itself. "Don't you remember the Suit's ship? It was bigger on the inside than it was on the outside. This is the same thing, only more so."

"The dimensional folding principle is the same," Dandelion interrupted, sounding and looking annoyed as she glanced over her shoulder, "but the technology is in no way comparable. Perhaps we could discuss it later, but something has come up that demands my immediate attention."

Turning back to the miniature keyboard, she tapped in a quick code, and the floor opened up under our feet. Everything glowed again for a second, and then the glow was floating upward, like a cloud of fluorescent yellow steam. In three or four seconds, it was gone and we were all standing in the grass behind the barn. For another second, a small, saucer-shaped yellow glow hovered a few feet above our heads, and then it too vanished.

"What was *that* all about?" I asked when I got my voice back.

"You'll get used to it," Uncle Harold said. "She always was zippin' off somewhere like that. You saw the way her collar glowed pink? That just meant she was gettin' a message from someone. Or some *thing*, like a booby trap she planted somewhere for your scaly pals, maybe. She was pretty good at booby traps, from what I remember."

"But why'd she yank us all inside her ship like that? Was somebody after us?"

Uncle Harold shrugged. "Maybe she just wanted you to see it," he said with a chuckle, "so you'd know for sure it wasn't anything like that other one you were in, the one the Daschkor lost."

Kathy frowned. "Just showing off, you mean?"

"Somethin' like that, maybe. Wants you to know she's drivin' a new Rolls Royce but the crooks are in a Model T."

He shrugged and looked up in the air where her "ship" had vanished. "Or maybe she had somethin' else altogether in mind. If you want the plain old truth of the matter, I've always had this funny feeling, way down inside somewhere, that she doesn't really trust me, not completely."

"That probably comes from her being a cat," Kathy said, "even an alien one like that. The ones here on Earth are nice enough, but I don't think they ever really trust anyone."

Uncle Harold snorted. "Considering what some people do to cats, you can't hardly blame them. And anyway, if you were on a planet where people were twenty times your size and all looked like giant tigers, would *you* trust anyone? Even a little bit?"

"If I had a collar like she has, I might," Kathy said. "That thing looks like it could get her out of just about anything."

"Maybe *that's* why she showed it to us," I said. "Maybe it was a warning not to mess around with her."

Uncle Harold nodded. "Wouldn't be a bit surprised. Showin' her claws, in a manner of speakin'."

"But she didn't take the invisibility gadget," I said, remembering what she'd been saying when whatever it

103

was had interrupted her. "And I'm pretty sure she was getting ready to."

"I was going to ask you about that," Uncle Harold said, his voice suddenly serious.

I reached into my pocket and pulled out the lumpy Baggie, but I almost dropped it when I saw that the gadget inside wasn't invisible anymore.

"Unless I missed somethin' in that little story you galloped through," Uncle Harold said, "you're not supposed to be able to see that gizmo."

"We couldn't see it," Kathy and I said, almost on top of each other.

But it was perfectly visible now. It was about the size and shape we'd figured it was by feeling it, about half the size of a Coke can, only lumpy and rectangular. The color was a sort of sickly green, like a big, square potato that was getting ready to mold. The lumps were slightly darker green, like they'd already molded.

"Does it still work?" Kathy asked.

"How should I know?"

"Let's find out," she said immediately.

I hesitated, remembering what Dandelion had said about its being dangerous in inexperienced hands. Hands didn't get much more inexperienced than ours.

"Maybe we should wait till she comes back," I said, "and she can show us how it's supposed to work."

"We already know how it works, Calvin! Remember? And now that we can see the thing, maybe—"

"Calvin's right, kiddo," Uncle Harold interrupted. "Like Dandelion said, you've both been pretty blamed lucky so far. And from what you were just sayin', it sounds like you've already been playin' around with this thing more than you should. Best not to push your luck too far. 'Specially if it's doin' things it's not supposed to do, like turnin' visible all of a sudden. Probably means another wire's come loose somewhere."

"But—"

"But me no buts, young lady. Nor you either, Nephew." He gave me one of those straight-in-the-eye looks that Mom uses now and then. This was the first time I'd ever seen Uncle Harold use one, and he was even better at it than Mom. I guess it was something else that ran in the family.

"Now, I don't know what makes that imitation feline tick," he went on, "and I'm not sure that I believe more'n about fifty-one percent of what she says. But if she says that gizmo you swiped could be dangerous, I figure she's got a better idea of what she's talkin' about than any of us do. Understand?"

I nodded, and after a few seconds so did Kathy. Reluctantly.

"So keep it in the sack," he said, "at least until she comes back. Don't go foolin' around with it any more than you already have."

Kathy was still reluctant, but she nodded again.

After a few seconds of silence, he took out his pocket watch—which apparently told time as well as detected aliens—and looked at it.

"Speaking of disappearing," he said, "it looks like we've disappeared for just about long enough. Your folks are probably gettin' ready to send out a search party."

As it turned out, though, they hadn't hardly noticed we were gone. Mom had found a half dozen of Aunt

Grace's dresses that she was sure were going to be back in style any day now, and she'd been trying them on to see if they could be made to fit. Dad, in another corner of the attic, had come across an ancient-looking book called *The History of Science*. According to Uncle Harold, *his* father had bought it from some door-to-door salesman back in the twenties, and Dad had been leafing through it for nearly an hour, shaking his head and chuckling every page or two. As for Walter, he had passed up a set of toy wooden soldiers for an ancient photo album and was exclaiming loudly whenever he came across another picture of Uncle Harold in short pants and broke into squealing laughter when he found one of him in a baby carriage.

That day, we stayed at Uncle Harold's longer than we usually did, practically the whole afternoon, and just before we left, he crammed us all into his Studebaker, a green antique so old it didn't even have safety belts, which didn't make Dad all that happy. It didn't bother Kathy, though, especially when she found out Uncle Harold was taking us into town for a taco burger at a fast-food place he knew about. (Until today, I would've been surprised that he even knew what fast foods were, let alone ate anything like a taco, but after hearing Dandelion call him Hal a half dozen times it didn't seem nearly as out of place.)

Anyway, it was nearly dark when we got back to East Gradwohl, and the invisibility gadget in my pocket was like that missing tooth you can't keep your tongue away from. Uncle Harold hadn't taken it away from me, just given me another warning to leave it alone until Dandelion showed up again.

"You got enough common sense to not do something dumb," he'd said, but I wasn't so sure myself, particularly with Kathy around. She gets straight A's and all that, and she's my best friend, but common sense isn't her strong point.

That evening, though, I was able to avoid at least the Kathy part of the problem, since my folks dropped her off at her place despite her protests. We'd been in the back seat all the way from Uncle Harold's, and from what she'd been whispering to me for most of the trip, it was pretty clear she wanted me to let her take the gadget home with her, and, to tell the truth, I don't know how much longer I could've held out. With her gone, there was just me to worry about, which was quite enough.

In my room, I took the Baggie out of my pocket and looked at the gadget inside. I even poked at some of the lumps through the plastic, but nothing happened, and eventually, when I went down to clean Hulk's litter pan, I took it to the basement and left it there, at the back of one of the more cluttered shelves, where nobody's looked for years. This way, I figured, even if the lizardy thing *did* come around again looking for his gadget, he'd be able to get it from the basement without coming up through the house like he'd probably tried to do last night when he'd gotten jumped by Hulk.

But nobody came that night, not unless they were a lot quieter and more professional about it than they had been the last time. I mean, so far as I know, there wasn't a sound all night. Hulk didn't do any prowling or growling, and when I woke up in the morning he was lying quietly on my feet the way he usually does, not a trace of green blood or anything else on his claws.

But I found out soon enough that things hadn't been quiet everywhere.

About eight-thirty, just after Dad left for work, the phone rang. I grabbed it up before Mom could get to it, figuring it would be Kathy. "Hello," I said.

"Calvin?" It wasn't Kathy's voice, but I couldn't figure out whose it was, just some man's.

"Yes," I said. "Who's this?"

"Your folks around?"

"Mom is. You want to talk to her?"

"No, just you. I'll pick you up in two shakes."

"Who—" I began again, but then, with the "two shakes," I realized who it was. "Uncle Harold?"

"Not so loud! Who'd you think it was, anyway? Now you just get ready. We ain't got any time to waste. Those lizards you were talkin' about yesterday, it looks like they got Dandelion."

11

"So That's How It Works."

Before I could ask more than a couple of the three or four dozen questions I wanted to ask—How do you know they've got her?, How can we help?, Is she all right?, Where are you?, that kind of thing—he'd hung up with another "Two shakes! You be outside, you hear me?"

I hung up, too, after a couple seconds staring at the phone. My first thought was that I didn't have the faintest idea what he meant by two shakes. He used it like other people used "in a little while" or "right away," which could be anywhere from five seconds to five weeks if the way he'd used it before was any example. But if he was still home—where else would he be calling from?—it would be a couple of hours, probably.

My second thought sent me galloping down the stairs to the basement, almost running into Mom, who was on the way back up after putting a load of laundry in the dryer. If they'd gotten Dandelion, I thought, maybe they'd gotten the invisibility gadget too, like they'd tried to do Saturday night.

But they hadn't. It was still in its Baggie on the shelf behind the half-empty buckets of paint left over from the last time we painted the garage.

And it was still visible, whatever that meant.

I stuffed it in my pocket and then had my third thought, which probably should've been my first. I called Kathy. I was just starting to tell her about Dandelion when a horn started blowing somewhere.

I looked out the window, and there was Uncle Harold in his green Studebaker, which meant, among other things, that he must've called from someplace besides home. It also meant that the situation was so urgent that he didn't really care if Mom heard him or not.

"Uncle Harold's here," I whispered into the phone. "We'll pick you up in a couple minutes."

I practically tripped over Mom, who'd been coming to the front to see who was honking.

"Who was that on the phone?" she asked.

"Kathy," I said, which wasn't really a lie.

"And I suppose that's where you're going in such a hurry?"

"Uh-huh," I said, nodding.

"Have you cleaned Hulk's litter pan this morning? And put out fresh water for him?"

I always did that stuff first thing when I got up, so I was okay there.

"I don't suppose you're going out to the Diefenbacher place again today, are you?" she asked, eyeing me suspiciously.

"Maybe," I said, hoping Uncle Harold didn't blow his horn again.

She kept looking at me suspiciously, but then there was a clatter from the kitchen. "Walter!" she said loudly, and then she was hurrying toward the sound.

I ducked out the front door, fast. Uncle Harold's green Studebaker wasn't across the street anymore, but as I was standing on the sidewalk, looking, there was another honk from near the end of the block.

When I climbed in, he looked a little sheepish. "I forgot you said your mother was home," he said. "Now—"

"We have to pick up Kathy," I said.

He broke off, frowning at me. "Your little friend? Why?"

"Because she'll probably have a lot better idea how to save Dandelion from those lizards than I will, that's why."

"Who said we were gonna try to save her?"

"You drove a hundred miles to get here. You must be going to try *something!*"

"I just want to find out where those lizards are hidin' out, that's all. You said it was called the Diddlebacher place, or somethin' like that."

"Diefenbacher," I said. "Is that where they took her?"

"How the blue blazes should I know? But if it ain't, I got no chance at *all* to help her. Probably ain't got *much* of a chance even if she *is* there."

"That's why we have to pick Kathy up. If it hadn't

been for her, we never would've been able to save that hairy tourist. The whole thing was her idea. Besides, I already told her we'd be over to get her."

He frowned at me. "And I s'pose you told her what I said about Dandelion?"

I nodded. "And if we don't come by, she'll probably start out to the Diefenbacher place on her bike. By herself."

"You couldn't just call her back and tell her—" He stopped and shook his head. "No, I don't s'pose that would do a lot of good," he said, and I thought I saw just the tiniest bit of a smile.

"Okay," he said with a sigh, "which way?"

Kathy, clutching a paper bag in one hand, was pacing back and forth on the corner a half block from her house when we got there. Without waiting for the car to completely stop, she yanked the door open and crowded in next to me in the front seat—which in a Studebaker isn't all that wide—and dumped the paper bag on the floor by her feet.

"What happened?" she asked before the door was slammed shut. "Where did they take her? The Diefenbacher place?"

"That's what I want to find out," Uncle Harold said. "Now if one of you'd be so kind as to tell me where this Diefenbacher place is, maybe I could get on with what I came for."

"It's five or six miles out of town," Kathy said, "but what *happened?*"

"You tell me which way to go, and I'll tell you what happened. Much's I saw, anyway."

"You go back this way," Kathy said, pointing, "to

Main, and then you turn right. Now what—" She broke off, swiveling in the seat to look at me. "Where's that gadget? You didn't leave it at home, did you?"

"It's in my pocket," I said, getting a quick frown from Uncle Harold as he pulled into a driveway and backed out heading the other way. "For all the good it'll do."

"You never know," she said with a touch of smugness. "Now what happened?"

"They were waitin' for her, it looks like," Uncle Harold said after a couple of seconds. "Tracked her down or somethin'. Anyway, I woke up last night, oh, around three o'clock. Heard this noise, the kinda noise her ship used to make. Not the one she's got now, but the one she had back then. I s'pose the new one's an improved model or something. A lot quieter, anyway."

He came to a stop at Main. "Now which way?"

We both pointed to the right.

"Anyway, I looked out the window, but I couldn't see anything. I even put on my clothes and went outside to look around, but there wasn't a thing." He shrugged. "I figured she'd show herself when she got good and ready. That's the way she usually does things. But then, just when I got back inside the house, there was this glow, you know the kind. You saw it yesterday yourself. Not a sound this time, so I started back outside again. And this time it *was* her. That ship of hers sort of melted away from around her the way it does, and started shrinkin' down to collar size."

"That first sound," Kathy said, "that had been another ship? Full of those lizards?"

"Not sure how full it was, but there must've been at least one, and he must've had a spare one of those gizmos you took away from them. Anyway, this thing that looked like a crocodile standin' up on its hind legs popped out of nowhere, right next to Dandelion. And he grabbed her ship. See, it hadn't shrunk all the way down yet, so she hadn't got it around her neck yet, where she could get at it right away. And then he grabbed *her*, and that was that. Then he hopped into a big green glow that showed up next to him the second he got his hands on Dandelion and her ship."

"And you think they took her to the Diefenbacher place?" Kathy asked.

Uncle Harold shrugged irritably. "Hopin's more like it," he said. "You got any better ideas what to do? Calvin here's been talkin' you up pretty good."

She shook her head. "If she's still on Earth, that's probably where she is. But how do we find out for sure?"

He tapped his watch pocket. "Brought along that dingus she gave me. Figure if we just drive by the place, that should be enough to get a reading."

"And if they're in there? What then?"

"Let *me* worry about that."

"I brought something that might help," Kathy said, picking up the paper bag she'd dropped on the floor when she climbed in.

"What's that?" I asked. Uncle Harold was concentrating on driving now.

Instead of saying anything, she opened the bag and pulled out a pair of little black boxes with metal antennas sticking out of them.

"Walkie-talkies?" I said. "What are we supposed to do with *them*?"

"You know how you go blind when you're invisible? Well, if you took one of these, maybe someone could guide you from a distance. I could see where you were by the dents your feet make in the ground, or something like that, and I could tell you which way to go."

For a second, it made sense, but only for a second.

In the first place, I doubted that I could get the whole walkie-talkie inside the field. The last time, even after we'd accidentally hit the right lumps and managed to expand it, the field had only extended a couple of inches out from our bodies, just about enough to include my hair and clothes. Some of Kathy's hair had still been outside. What we'd probably end up with, unless we could figure out how to expand the thing even more, would be about half of a walkie-talkie floating in midair, which wouldn't be all that inconspicuous.

But then I thought of the second place. "It wouldn't work," I said.

"How do you know, Mr. Spock? Have you tried it?"

"No, but I don't have to try it. That thing makes you invisible by making you transparent to light waves, right? Well, radio waves are the same as light waves, only longer, so it probably makes you transparent to radio waves too. If you had an invisible walkie-talkie with you, it couldn't pick up any messages."

"Are you sure?" she asked, frowning.

"Pretty sure," I said.

"Let's find out. Here, you take one," she said, handing me one of the little machines. "And give me the invisibility gadget."

"Now, hold your horses a minute," Uncle Harold said when I started to pull the gadget out of my pocket.

But instead of taking it away from me or ordering us to leave it alone, he pulled off to the side of the road.

"Let me see that gizmo," he said as the car came to a stop.

With a glance at Kathy, I handed it to him.

"Now all you do is touch it and you disappear?" he said, fingering the Baggie it was in.

"That's how it worked when it was invisible itself," I said.

Gingerly, he opened the Baggie.

And touched the gadget.

Nothing happened.

"It's broken," Kathy said, sounding annoyed.

Uncle Harold took the gadget out of the Baggie, and still nothing happened. "What are all those lumps?" he asked.

"They *might* be controls," I said.

Cautiously, he poked a finger at the biggest, moldiest-looking lump.

The gadget flickered and disappeared, and a second later so did Uncle Harold.

And so did about three inches of the car's seat under him and behind him, leaving severed ends of springs visible, along with all the brown and gray and white junk that made up the cushions.

An instant later, there was a gasp and something fell into my lap. Another instant later, Uncle Harold and the rest of the front seat reappeared.

I automatically grabbed at whatever had hit my lap, and everything went black. Blindly, I fumbled for the Baggie, found it, and dropped the gadget inside.

A second later, I could see again.

"So that's how it works," Uncle Harold said. He sounded shaky.

"If you two are through playing games," Kathy said, "maybe we can find out if the walkie-talkies work."

So we tried. We even found a way to get the walkie-talkies all the way—well, almost all the way—inside the field. What you had to do was sort of sandwich it between your hand and your head so that it was half in the field around your head and half in the field made by your hand. That way, all that showed was the antenna and a couple little patches where the fields didn't quite overlap, and if you angled it just right even the antenna disappeared. I stayed in the car with Uncle Harold and got invisible while Kathy took her walkie-talkie a few feet away, outside the car. I had my own walkie-talkie pressed to my ear in the darkness.

To my surprise, something did come through, but it was mostly static, and it happened only when Kathy was trying to talk to me. Likewise, when I tried to talk to her she picked up extra static, too, but that wasn't a lot of help. Guiding somebody by turning static on and off didn't sound too practical, especially since neither one of us knew Morse Code.

With the walkie-talkies back in their bag, Uncle Harold pulled back out on the road, and a few minutes later we were cruising past the Diefenbacher place. He had his watch in one hand while he steered with the other.

"Nothing there," he said when we were a good quarter of a mile past, turning into the first driveway we'd come to. "Not the slightest tingle." He was quiet a few seconds before backing out onto the blacktop road.

117

"I'm goin' in there and see if I can find anything," he said, putting the car in gear. "You kids stay in the car."

"Are you sure nobody's in there?" Kathy asked. "I mean, maybe that gadget of yours isn't working. Remember what Dandelion said about it? That Walter could never have been 'permanently turned on' by it? But he was, and if it could goof up that way, it could be goofing up some other way now."

"So what do you suggest, young lady?"

"I suggest we go back and get Walter and drive by the place with *him*."

Uncle Harold gave her a squinty look that wasn't all that encouraging. "And *I* suggest we go back and I drop you two off and we forget about the whole thing," he said.

I didn't say anything. To tell the truth, I agreed with Uncle Harold. I mean, when we went out to the Diefenbacher place the first couple of times, we didn't really know what we were doing or what we were getting into. But now . . . Well, we still didn't *know* what we were getting into, but it was a lot more serious than what we'd thought the first time. And we *sure* didn't know what we were *doing*, and dragging Walter into something like that didn't seem like the brightest thing in the world to do.

So I let Kathy do all the arguing, and for once she got nowhere at all, not even when she threatened to take her bike and haul Walter out here on the handlebars. Uncle Harold was showing a tougher side than I'd ever seen him show before.

"You even *think* about something like that, young lady," he said, "and I'll figure out some way of gettin' you grounded for a month! And I'll have it figured out by the time we get you home, too, don't think I won't!"

But when we got home, the situation changed, radically.

Uncle Harold pulled up right in front of our house. "Remember what I said," he said. "Don't do anything dumb, either one of you."

Kathy and I both nodded, Kathy a little more reluctantly than me.

"And maybe you better give me that gizmo," he added.

"What are you going to do with it?" Kathy asked sharply.

"Nothin'," he said. "Or maybe I'll drive by that place and toss it out. I don't know. Depends on how I feel."

My own guess—and probably Kathy's—was that he would go back out to the Diefenbacher place to look around, just the way he'd been planning to do all along, hoping he could find something that would help him figure out what had happened to Dandelion.

Anyway, as Kathy and I got out of the Studebaker, I pulled the Baggie out of my pocket and started to hand it to him while Kathy reached in the back and got her bag of walkie-talkies. But before he took the Baggie from me, our front screen door slammed open.

And Walter came running out like some monster was chasing him.

"Calvin!" he screamed, and I do mean screamed, at the top of his lungs. "Somebody was here! Somebody was here and took Mom!"

12

"Something I Really Didn't Want to Hear."

Uncle Harold was out of the car, moving faster than I'd ever seen him move, and then he was kneeling down, grabbing Walter's shoulders and looking him straight in the face.

"*Who* was here, Walter? What happened?"

Walter gulped loudly, his eyes going back and forth between me and Uncle Harold. "I—I don't know! I didn't see them!"

"That's okay," Uncle Harold said, putting his arms around Walter. "We'll get things straightened out in a jiffy, okay?" He paused, patting the boy on the back. "Now, you just take it easy, kiddo. Get ahold of yourself and tell us whatever you can."

"It was like when Hulk got in that fight," he said. "It was—"

"Saturday night, you mean?" I asked. "When the stuff got knocked over downstairs."

He nodded emphatically. "I was scared, but there wasn't anything to be scared of."

"A sort of tingly feeling?" Uncle Harold asked. "Kind of like chills all over your skin, maybe even inside you?"

Walter's eyes widened. "How'd you know? Do you get scared like that, too?"

"It's happened," Uncle Harold said, glancing down in the general direction of his watch pocket. "What happened next? You said somebody came to the house."

"Somebody was at the back door," he said. "They were knocking, real hard, and Mom— I didn't want her to go, but—"

"But she didn't pay any attention to you, and she went and answered the door anyway. What happened then?"

"I was *really* scared then, and I ran out into the front yard, and—and when I came back in, she wasn't there!"

"Did you hear anything?"

Walter shook his head.

"No hissing or anything like that? Right before you started to get scared?"

Again Walter shook his head. "I didn't hear *anything!*"

"Did anyone come inside the house?"

"I don't know!" Walter almost wailed, and then Uncle Harold had his arms around him again.

"That's okay, kiddo," he said. "That's okay. Everything's going to be all right."

"But where's *Mommy?*"

"I told you, we'll find her and we'll have her back in two shakes." Uncle Harold moved back, his hands still on Walter's shoulders. "But you may have to help us. Okay?"

Walter just nodded, still gulping occasionally.

As for me—well, I was probably feeling about the way Walter was, kind of sick, and like all of a sudden the whole world was a very scary place. Even Kathy wasn't saying a word, but from the way she was gritting her teeth it looked like she was more mad than scared.

Then Uncle Harold was looking at me and Kathy. "You two know better than me how things are here in East Gradwohl," he said. "What would happen if we went to that Sheriff Pippenger with all this?"

"Nothing good," Kathy said instantly. "Even if he believed us—"

"With that gizmo in Calvin's pocket, we could make him believe us, all right. Once one of us disappeared right in front of his eyes, he'd believe us."

I shook my head. "Who knows what he'd believe? He'd probably think *we* were monsters from outer space. Or he'd call in the National Guard to surround the Diefenbacher place or something like that, just like he did with that tourist in the rock."

Uncle Harold was real quiet for a second or two, looking like he was thinking really hard.

"Okay," he said abruptly, "I guess that wouldn't really help matters all that much. Looks like we don't have a lot of choice." He looked down at Walter again. "How about you, kiddo? You still feel like givin' us a hand?"

Walter bobbed his head up and down in a huge nod.

So we all got in the green Studebaker, me in the front hanging on to Walter, Kathy in the back.

Nobody said a word until we were in sight of the Diefenbacher place.

"Maybe you'll start feeling scared in a minute or

two," I said to Walter then, "like you did before. But don't worry about it. Just tell us if it happens, that's all."

But he didn't have to say anything. When we were still a couple hundred yards down the road, I could feel him start to shiver.

Not only that, I started to feel some of the tingling myself, and I started wondering if I was imagining things. But then, when I let go of Walter's bare arms for a second, the tingling went away, and I realized what was really happening.

Whatever it was Walter had, it was contagious, like the invisibility. That watch of Uncle Harold's had turned *him* on permanently, and now he was able to turn other people on, but only as long as he was touching them.

"Whatever they are, they're in there," I said, pointing at the Diefenbacher place as we went by.

The car speeded up and didn't stop until we came to the same driveway we'd turned around in the first time we were out here, and for a second I thought I saw someone looking out a window in the house twenty or thirty yards back from the road.

We sat there, nobody saying a thing, just looking back in the direction of the Diefenbacher place, for maybe a minute.

Finally Walter looked around at me. "Is Mommy back there?" he asked.

"Looks that way," Uncle Harold said, glancing first at Walter, then at Kathy and me. "Now all we got to do is get her—and Dandelion—out."

"Any ideas?" I asked. "What were you planning on doing when it was just Dandelion?"

"Not real sure," he admitted. He reached down and pulled two packs of cigarettes out of the glove compartment. "I stopped and bought these along the way, so I guess I figured if I got close enough, I could knock 'em all out with the smoke."

"Smoke would do that?" Kathy leaned forward over the back of the seat.

"Accordin' to what Dandelion told me way back when, it sure would. Remember what she called my smoking—a 'deadly habit' or somethin' like that? Thing is, to her and most others from out there, it really is deadly. Pure poison. Not that it ain't poison to us too, but to them it's a lot faster. Acts like nerve gas or something on them. Earth's the only planet she knows of that has anything quite like tobacco. Anyway, the gizmos they use for breathin' our atmosphere clean out enough of it so they can get along in the open air, but that's why they hardly ever go inside buildings with a lot of people. They get a puff of smoke right in their face, it might not knock them out, but it'd be like a whiff of ammonia to us."

"And you figured if you could get close enough, you could blow smoke in their faces?"

"Somethin' like that."

"But how were you going to get close enough?"

"Hadn't figured that part out yet. Unless maybe all us humans look alike to them, and I could just walk up to the front door." He shook his head. "Too bad your walkie-talkie idea won't work. You could've steered me right up to the door that way."

Suddenly Kathy brightened. "Calvin and I—"

"Now just a minute!" he interrupted, not even wait-

ing to see what Kathy's idea was. "Without those cigarettes, you ain't got a chance, and I'm pretty blame sure
neither one of you smokes."

"We don't have to! Calvin, you remember how when
you touch someone who's invisible, you disappear
yourself?"

"Sure, but—"

"Well, how about if we *both* go up there. You hang on
to the cigarettes and a—" She looked at Uncle Harold.
"You do have something to light them with, don't you?"

He pulled a massive lighter out of the glove compartment. "Got the biggest one they had," he said.
"And a pocketful of matches just to be on the safe side,"
he added, patting one of his pockets.

"Okay." Kathy went on, her words rushing out.
"Now, Calvin, you carry the cigarettes and the lighter
and the invisibility gadget, and I'll hold on to your
hand, and we can sort of crawl along through the
weeds, there's plenty of those around there, and every
so often I can let go of your hand, you know, for just a
half a second or something like that, so I can see where
we are, and then I'll grab your hand and get invisible
again, and that way we can get right up to the house,
and they'll never even see us."

"It might work," I said, "but what do we do then?"

"We look through the windows—*I* look through the
windows the same way, just letting go of you for a half
second. When we find out where they're keeping your
mom and Dandelion, we go inside the same way, or
maybe we make some noise around the front door and I
let them see me and when they come out, you're still
invisible and you have a fistful of cigarettes lit and you

throw them when I tell you to. Or something like that. Maybe first we should just scout the place out, you know, just look through the windows and see where they're at, and then we can come back here and figure out exactly what to do."

"I don't like it," Uncle Harold said.

"Do you have a better idea?" Kathy asked.

"I'll just walk up there," he said halfheartedly. "They probably *can't* tell one human from another."

But in the end, we tried it Kathy's way. If that didn't work, we'd try something else.

If we were still able.

For five or ten minutes, I fiddled with the lighter until I could light a half-dozen cigarettes in a few seconds with my eyes closed while holding one end of the invisibility gadget in my mouth, which was the only way I could use both hands for the lighting. The major problem was to keep from choking and coughing and spitting out the invisibility gadget. Another problem was that when Kathy let go of my hand and became visible, she had trouble finding it again, so we took one of Uncle Harold's shoestrings and tied our wrists together, kind of like mountain climbers tie themselves together with a rope, only loose enough so that if Kathy wanted to become permanently visible and distract them, she could slip it off in a second.

Then Uncle Harold parked the car on the other side of some trees, out of sight of the Diefenbacher place. A few yards down the road, though, he could scrunch down in the ditch and watch us all the way.

And we started. Before getting invisible, we picked a place we hoped was out of sight from the house and climbed over the fence. Then we pretty much crawled, really slowly, down in the weeds and stuff, feeling our way along. Every minute or so, Kathy would stick her head up like a periscope to about what she figured was the top of the weeds and let go of my hand for an instant. Usually, then, we'd change direction a little, like to get around a tree or something, and then crawl some more. I was really glad things had dried off since that first day we were out there, although the burrs and stickers and things we kept running into were bad enough.

After a couple dozen sightings, we had another piece of real luck and found a whole section of the fence missing, and by the next time Kathy put up her periscope, we were in the yard itself.

"We've only got fifteen or twenty feet to go!" she whispered in my ear. "Then I can start looking in the windows! I just hope your Uncle Harold holds off long enough for us to get something done!"

After another five or ten feet, however, I heard something I didn't really want to hear. It sounded very much like there was something besides the two of us out there creeping through the weeds, and whatever it was, it was coming closer.

And then there was something I absolutely hated to hear. It was a voice, and it was practically on top of us. It also didn't sound all that human, the way it hissed its s's. Worst of all, however, was what it said:

"You can stop all this foolishness any time you feel like it. We can see you—and your Uncle Harold— quite well."

13

"Get in Here, You Boneheads!"

The first thing I felt was Kathy's hand squeezing mine so hard my fingers hurt. I squeezed back, probably just as hard, and tried to keep as quiet as possible there in the blackness. I even held my breath. I don't know whether I figured the voice was lying or what, or maybe that its owner couldn't really see us but had just seen the grass moving and was guessing where we were.

But whatever I figured, I found out about two seconds later that I was wrong. There hadn't been any guessing involved. The voice obviously knew exactly where I was, because the next thing it did was turn into a hand and grab the invisibility gadget away from me.

All of a sudden I could see again.

Except for whatever had grabbed the gadget away from me, of course.

There was no one in the yard—no one visible, that is—except Kathy and me.

"You two are becoming quite troublesome," the hissing voice said, and it came from only two or three feet away.

We both looked toward the sound, but we couldn't see anything—except a pair of dents an inch or two deep in the ground. The dents looked kind of like footprints made by a big lizard, and they were right in the middle of a spot a couple feet across where the grass and the weeds were pushed aside and flattened down. Like something was standing there.

Then something grabbed my free hand, something scaly and scratchy. At the same time, my hand disappeared up to the wrist. At least, I didn't disappear altogether, which I guess meant that whatever had grabbed me must have had some kind of glove on. Either that or those scales on its hand were dead, like our hair, and couldn't conduct the field.

Anyway, whatever it was practically took my arm off yanking me to my feet. I squeaked or made some other kind of undignified noise and pulled back. Kathy, who so far hadn't made a sound, now let out a yell and scrambled to her feet and aimed a kick at the air above the foot-shaped dents.

Whatever had hold of my hand got even tighter, and the two foot-shaped dents disappeared and reappeared a couple of feet to one side. And Kathy gave my other hand a yank.

"Let's go!" she said, slipping her wrist out of the shoestring.

"I can't! It's got me!" I said, still squeaking. Inspired by Kathy, I tried some kicking myself.

And my shoe hit something.

But after that, things only got worse.

First, the invisible grip on my invisible hand got even tighter, and a second later I realized I couldn't move at all. I couldn't even talk.

And because Kathy quit pulling me, I figured she must be in the same condition I was.

"Come," the voice said, and all of a sudden I was being pulled along, sort of stumbling, toward the front door, following the foot-shaped dents as they alternately appeared and disappeared. Kathy was still hanging on to my other hand, and she was following right along behind me.

Some kind of controller, I thought, like a cattle prod for people, and I wondered if Uncle Harold was seeing all this and what he would—or could—do about it if he was.

Then we were inside, in the big room at the foot of the stairs. Dandelion was standing motionless by the stairs, and next to her, sitting on the bottom step just as motionless, was Mom.

"Calvin!" Mom said, but only her mouth and eyes moved. "Kathy? What happened? What *are* these things?"

I tried to answer her, but I still couldn't talk. Kathy and I were stopped just a couple of feet from her, and we felt ourselves sitting down on the floor.

Whatever had been hanging on to my hand let go.

My hand reappeared.

And I could talk again.

But before I could say anything, a lizard sort of like the one I'd seen out here a couple of days ago appeared out of thin air three or four feet in front of us. It was purplish green instead of grayish green, and it had something that looked very much like Dandelion's collar around its scaly wrist. It also had a half-dozen grayish metallic-looking straps wrapped around it like belts or bandoleers.

It looked over its shoulder toward the door to the kitchen. "Get in here, you boneheads!" it half shouted.

After a few seconds, two more of the dinosaurish-looking lizards peered around the edge of the door and then crept through. They were more grayish green than purplish green, and the way they moved reminded me of the way a dog creeps into a room after someone's yelled at it.

"Here," the purplish one said, tossing the invisibility gadget he'd taken from me—it was visible again—toward them. One ducked back into the kitchen, but the other one caught it.

And disappeared instantly, along with the gadget itself.

There was a clattering sound, and he reappeared, but the invisibility gadget didn't. With a nervous glance at the nearby lizard, the one that had reappeared dropped to its knees and began patting the floor, about the way Kathy had done when she'd found the invisibility gadget in the first place. The nearby one gave a hissing snort, which only made the one on the floor scramble around faster and make a tiny squealing sound, almost like a large mouse, or maybe one of the Three Stooges. If it had been louder, it would've sounded pretty much like the noises Kathy and I had heard on the other side of that locked door that first day we were out here.

Then the one that had ducked into the kitchen tiptoed back into the room, and I could hear the scratchy toenails sound we'd heard that first day. About the third step, he let out a full-size squeal and disappeared just as quickly as the other one had.

He also reappeared, even more quickly, hopping on one foot. He must've stepped on the gadget, and the one on his hands and knees lunged toward where the other one was hopping around and began pounding the floor all around him. After a half-dozen pounds, he too vanished, but without the squeal.

The purplish one, still standing in front of Kathy and me, let out another hissing snort and stalked across the room. Reaching down, he grabbed a handful of something and disappeared. He was gone for ten or fifteen seconds, and then he was back, along with the other one. He was holding the invisibility gadget—visible once again—in one hand and gripping the other lizard's arm with his other hand.

With a final hissing snort, he led—almost dragged— the other two into the kitchen. His purplish head reappeared in the door for a second as he gave the four of us a look that was probably the lizard equivalent of a scowl, and then he was gone. A second later, all kinds of squealing sounds—this time almost exactly like what had been on the other side of that locked door the other day—broke out.

"Remarkable, truly remarkable," Dandelion's high-pitched, silky voice said. "What did you two *do* to that device of theirs?"

Before Kathy or I could say anything—not that either of us had anything helpful to say—there was another squeak, this time from Mom. "*It* talks, *too?*" she said.

"Of course I talk," Dandelion said, sounding slightly miffed.

"It's a long story, Mrs. Willeford," Kathy said. "Right now, we have to figure out how to get out of here."

"But—" Mom began.

"Quite correct, young lady," Dandelion said. "I doubt that we are in any *real* danger from those creatures—they're Mildrolfans, by the way, almost as backward as the Daschkor—but it is best not to take unnecessary chances."

"She's from outer space, Mom," I said, as quickly as I could, "like that thing they saw at school. And so are those lizards that were just in here. We'll tell you all about it later. Like Kathy said, right now we have to figure out how to get out of here."

"But why are they *doing* this to us?" Mom asked. "And what *can* we do? We're *paralyzed!*"

"They are hoping to influence me through you," Dandelion said. "That is all. They know I cannot allow harm to come to you, and Craystock wishes me to—"

"Craystock?" That was Kathy.

"He is their leader, the one who brought the two of you inside just now. I do not recognize his bumbling assistants. But as I was saying, Craystock wishes me to return the ship I took from his assistants several days ago, but of course I cannot. As for the seeming para-

133

lysis, that is nothing to concern yourselves about. Craystock is merely using my own restraining field on us. You can think of it as being rather like your handcuffs, but far more advanced. And totally harmless, of course."

"I don't suppose you know how to pick the lock?" Kathy whispered.

"Rest assured, I have been working on the problem."

"But you haven't succeeded?"

"Not yet," Dandelion said, sounding slightly subdued. "Normally the field's own safety devices would allow me to override any commands given by someone other than myself."

"Normally? You mean it isn't working normally now?"

She hesitated, her fur riffling. "It is most odd and disconcerting," she said, almost as if talking to herself. "I wonder if this problem could be related to the odd behavior of their cloaking device."

"Cloaking device? You mean the invisibility gadget?" I asked.

"Yes. It too appears to be operating quite erratically."

"Yeah," Kathy said. "For one thing, I don't think it made us completely invisible while we were trying to sneak up here. That one lizard, Craystock or whoever, could still see us."

"That is not what I meant." Dandelion sniffed. "He was *supposed* to be able to see you. The device is designed to make the user transparent to only that range of electromagnetic energy which the planet's *natives* utilize for vision. On Earth that of course means the spectrum to which human eyes—your eyes—respond. Mildrolfan eyes are sensitive to other wavelengths. The device would hardly be of any use if it made its users blind."

Which would've made me feel a little silly if I'd had the time. I mean, I should've thought of it myself. It's only logical that a lizard's eyes would be different from a human's. And it's *certainly* logical that they wouldn't use a gadget that made them blind.

But then I remembered the walkie-talkie. It didn't operate anywhere near the spectrum of visible light, but it hadn't worked inside the field.

"What about lower frequencies," I asked, "down where radios and things operate?"

"They should not be affected to any great extent," Dandelion said impatiently. "There would be a minor frequency shift, but that is normally all."

So that was it! I thought. No wonder we'd gotten only static. With the frequency of the signal shifted like that, it would be like tuning your radio just to one side of the station you wanted to get. You'd pick up just enough noise to know there was a signal there, but that was all.

"The way the device is working now, however," Dandelion was going on, "there is no way of knowing *what* has been happening. For instance, it made them transparent to virtually the entire spectrum from deep infrared to far ultraviolet, including every wavelength to which their own eyes are sensitive. That is why they were fumbling around like a herd of Daschkor."

Kathy frowned. "How do *you* know what it did?"

"I could see it, of course. My own eyes encompass the entire human and Mildrolfan spectrum and more. The point, however, is that the device *did* malfunction.

135

Just as the safety override of my own restraining field appears to have malfunctioned. That is a remarkable coincidence—if it is indeed a coincidence."

I would've shrugged, except my shoulders didn't work any better than anything else below my neck. "It's like I said, these outer-space gadgets are always breaking down."

"I assume you are referring again to the devices belonging to that hairy lummox you saved," Dandelion said, managing to sound slightly resentful.

"That's right. None of his stuff worked, either. His disguise gadget broke down. The gadget that translated his language broke down. The gadget that was supposed to lead him back to his ship had broken down before we even met him. The gadget that kept him breathing broke down."

Dandelion was silent for a moment, as if my list had set her to thinking. "That *does* seem excessive, even for a Daschkor. And now my *own* equipment—"

"And don't forget that detector you left with Uncle Harold," Kathy said. "That conked out, too, and it turned Walter into a permanent detector."

"You are positive of that?"

"Positive," I put in. "Uncle Harold drove past this place just now using the detector himself, and he couldn't feel a thing, but then we came by with Walter and he knew right away there were aliens in here. And last week, he knew whenever one of those Dashers or whatever was around. And two nights ago, when one of these lizards broke into our house, he could feel *that* too."

I'd glanced toward Mom while I was talking, wondering how she was taking the news that Walter was outside with Uncle Harold, but she was looking calmer than I'd expected.

Dandelion gave us another moment of silence and another fur riffle, which she was somehow still able to do despite the "restraining field."

"Perhaps you are right," she said finally. "And now that I take the time to consider it, I can see that there is also the matter of my ship and the way in which it was taken from me. The mass drainage and the dimensional folding did seem to proceed more slowly than they should have. Had those processes been operating at normal speed, that creature could never have snatched my ship from me during the transition."

Suddenly, Kathy got that I've-got-an-idea look on her face. "Does this sort of thing *always* happen to you people? Every time you come to Earth, I mean?"

"Of course not! Nothing like this has *ever* happened to me! On Earth or on any other planet!"

"And you've been here a lot?"

"A number of times, yes."

"And this detector of yours, and the—the force-field handcuffs and that collar of yours that turns into a ship—those are the only things that have ever broken down?"

"They have hardly 'broken down'! But, yes, to the best of my knowledge those are the only devices of mine that have been the victim of even *minor* malfunctions."

By now Kathy was grinning from ear to ear, the way

she does when she's figured something out, but I didn't have the faintest idea what it could be or what good it could do us.

"Kathy—" I began, but she cut me off.

"Calvin! Don't you *see?*"

"See? See what?"

"The *reason* all those things are breaking down! It's as plain as—"

But whatever it was as plain as, we didn't have a chance to find out, at least not right then, because that's when someone started pounding on the front door.

Uncle Harold! I thought. He must've seen us become visible and walk inside, and he must've figured something had gone wrong, so he decided to take a chance and just walk up to the front door, like he'd wanted to do in the first place.

But why knock? Why warn them he was there? Unless he had Walter pounding on the door while he ducked around to the back, and—

Then we saw the reason for the pounding on the front door.

It wasn't Uncle Harold *or* Walter.

It was Sheriff Pippenger, and he was holding his face close to the window and peering inside.

Meanwhile, the squeaking argument—if that's what it was that had been going on hot and heavy in the kitchen ever since the three lizards had stepped out there—had stopped abruptly, and there was the sound of toenails clicking in our direction.

But it wasn't one of the lizards that appeared in the door to the kitchen. It was a human.

More or less.

Obviously one of the lizards, probably Craystock, had turned on his disguise gadget. The result looked more realistic than the Suits had, but it was still wearing a black suit and hat. And despite the shoes the image was wearing, you could hear toenails clicking on the floor as it walked to the front door and opened it.

"Come in," it said in a voice that was at least as human as that of the other Suits we'd talked to. "We have been expecting you, Uncle Harold."

"That's not—" I began, but Kathy shushed me violently.

I shushed, realizing that Uncle Harold had been right after all. The lizards *couldn't* tell one human from another. But what was *Pippenger* doing here, anyway?

And where *was* Uncle Harold?

14

"I Think We've All Been Kidnapped by Monsters from Outer Space."

"Sorry to bother you," Pippenger said as he stepped inside. "I'm the county sheriff, and I just received a call from one of your neighbors about some suspicious characters lurking in your—"

That was when he saw not just Kathy and me but Mom.

He looked confused.

And he turned sharply to look behind him. "Mr. Clayton," he said, which was Uncle Harold's last name, "why didn't you tell me that Mrs. Willeford—"

He stopped, the confusion turning into a frown. "Mr. Clayton, where *are* you?" he called as he stepped back onto the porch and looked around. "I'm warning you!" he shouted. "Whatever you're up to, you're not going to get away with it!"

But Uncle Harold was apparently nowhere in sight,

and a second later I heard a choking cough and I realized where he was and what he was doing. He was almost all the way around the house to the back door, and he was lighting a cigarette.

Meanwhile, the disguised lizard was fidgeting around, looking as if he was trying to figure out what to do now that Pippenger had gone back out on the porch. From the kitchen came a few more squeaks and toenails, and from outside came another cough, this one even closer to the back door.

"Dandelion," I began, intending to warn her about Uncle Harold's smoke, but before I could say any more the back door burst open and Uncle Harold stumbled into the kitchen, not one cigarette in his mouth but four.

I couldn't see the two kitchen lizards, but there was a flurry of toenails again and a burst of even louder squeaks. Uncle Harold looked stunned for just a second—seeing a pair of grayish-green lizards like that, even if you have been warned, can affect you that way—but then he inhaled deeply and lurched across the room toward the toenails.

There was even more toenail scrabbling and squeaking as he disappeared into a part of the kitchen I couldn't see, and a half second later there was a fit of coughing followed by a couple of even higher-pitched squeaks and a pair of solid thuds.

Meanwhile, Pippenger had heard the kitchen commotion and had come charging back in from the porch, brushing past the disguised and dithering lizard still in the room with the rest of us.

141

"Clayton!" Pippenger yelled as he crossed the floor. "What the blue blazes do you think—"

And that's as far as he got.

That's when the disguised lizard quit dithering. One hand reached inside his other wrist—inside the *image* of his other wrist—and made some sort of adjustment. An instant later Pippenger wasn't running and shouting anymore. His feet and tongue both stopped at the same time, and he hit the floor with a thump and ended up on one side, facing the wall next to the doorway to the kitchen.

About the same time, there was another thump, this one from the kitchen, and then I saw Uncle Harold's head and shoulders through the door. He was on the floor, too, and he still had three of the four cigarettes in his mouth.

"They have been caught in the restraining field," Dandelion said when I gave her a startled look.

The only thing moving now in either room was the disguised lizard, and he wasn't moving much. Mostly he was looking at Pippenger and then circling around to where he could get a look into the kitchen without having to go too near the door.

Pippenger apparently got his voice back about then, because that's when he started swearing.

"Is your little brother still out there?" Dandelion asked in a silky whisper that the lizard probably couldn't hear. "Do you think he will be coming in, too?"

"Now just a minute—" Mom began in a loud voice, but cut herself off when the lizard looked toward her.

"He might," I whispered back to Dandelion, "but the way things are going, I hope he doesn't."

"Do not be concerned. He could be just what we need. Try moving."

As the disguised lizard tiptoed back across the room and edged toward Pippenger's fallen form, I tried moving something besides my mouth and head.

To my surprise, I could. All I could do was wiggle my fingers, but that was more than I'd been able to do before. "What's happening?" I asked.

"They are stretching the limits of my restraining device," she said. "Even when it is working perfectly, it is meant to fully restrain only two or three culprits at a time. That is why they have relaxed a portion of the control so that we are able to speak. In that way, they are able to spread the field's energy farther and control at least the major movements of the six of us. If it has to control one more, however, it will most likely be spread so thin that I will be able to overcome it."

"Or it might break down altogether," I said.

"Until today, I would have said that was highly unlikely, but now I am not so sure."

Meanwhile, Pippenger had quit swearing and was asking more and more loudly what was going on.

After a half dozen or so times, Mom said something like "I wish I knew, Sheriff," and then added, "I think we've all been kidnapped by monsters from outer space."

And then, as if it had been waiting for the announcement, the lizard's disguise gadget apparently went crazy. He was tiptoeing past Pippenger, just getting into the sheriff's field of view, when it happened, and I can imagine what Pippenger was thinking. I mean, one second this guy in a black suit was clickily tiptoeing past him to get to the kitchen, and the next second the guy was replaced by a purplish-green lizard.

But to make matters worse, at least for Pippenger, Craystock was immediately replaced by something that looked like a five-foot-tall grasshopper, which was replaced almost as quickly by something seven feet high with slimy tentacles all over it. Then Craystock was back, a purplish-green lizard with a half-dozen lumpy grayish metallic belts and bandoleers strung all over its body, and this time it stayed that way. The disguise gadget must've died entirely after that last spasm.

"Craystock!" Dandelion said, as loudly as her silky voice could manage. "I really think you should stop all this foolishness and let us go before it's too late for you. Before you do something that will get you into *real* trouble."

Craystock made some squeaking noises, but only three or four English words came through, and none of them made any sense.

"Does that mean his translation whatchamacallit's broken?" Kathy asked excitedly. "He can't understand us anymore?"

"In all likelihood, yes," Dandelion said. "Do you—"

"I knew it!" Kathy said, and if she had been able to move she'd have been hopping up and down.

"Knew what?" Mom and I and Dandelion almost chorused.

"Don't you see, Calvin? Mrs. Willeford? It's what I

144

was starting to say when the sheriff showed up. It's *you* that's making things break down!"

"Us?" That was us.

"Them?" That was Dandelion.

"Yes! Calvin's been that way all his life, and he says you have, too, Mrs. Willeford. And Walter. You know how you have trouble with the car, and then when Calvin's dad shows up it works fine. Or the electronic timer on your stove you were having trouble with the other day. And how digital watches will never work for you, and all that stuff Calvin's always telling me about. And I'll bet your Uncle Harold is the same way! Machines just naturally break down around the whole bunch of you! But the thing right now is, if you all just concentrate real hard, maybe you can make that handcuff thing break down and we can all get loose!"

"That's crazy!" I started to say, but the words sort of faded away. I mean, with lizards from outer space kidnapping you and cats from outer space trying to rescue you, being told you have a hereditary something that makes machines malfunction is small potatoes.

Besides, right then something else flashed through my head, something that Dad had been talking about not long ago, and I all of a sudden realized that what Kathy was saying might even make some kind of logical sense. Dad had been talking about the way the microchips they were using in his designs at work were getting smaller every year, and he'd said that if they kept on getting smaller they'd have to start worrying about the "observer/observed interaction."

And then he'd explained a little bit—or a lot, really,

145

which is the way he does when he gets going on something he's interested in. See, it all has something to do with stuff called "quantum mechanics" and "new physics." It's starting to look, he said, like people's minds actually have some physical effect on what's happening way down there with the electrons and things. Not telepathy or telekinesis or anything like that, but . . .

Well, to tell the truth, I didn't really understand a lot of what he was saying, except that scientists—*real* scientists—are starting to say that electrons and subatomic particles and things like that really can be affected by what people think about them. And now, all of a sudden, I thought of a couple of other things.

First, if the subatomic stuff in those microchips that are in practically everything that's built these days *does* get changed when people think about it, even unconsciously, the changes could cause the chips to break down.

And, second, some people might just have more of an effect on that stuff than other people do.

People whose watches and TV sets and cars, all of which have all sorts of microchips in them these days, break down more often than other people's.

People like Mom and me.

Maybe, just maybe, Mom and I and Uncle Harold and Walter really *are* people like that. Maybe it—whatever "it" was—runs in the family, like Kathy said. Maybe what she was saying was sort of logical. After all, all these outer-space gadgets that keep breaking down must be filled with stuff even smaller and more complicated than microchips, so they'd be even more

146

likely to get goofed up if somebody aimed the wrong kinds of thoughts at them.

And if we could believe Dandelion, the only time her equipment ever broke down was when it was around someone in our family. Mom's side of the family, at least.

Anyway, a real jumbled, abbreviated version of all that stuff shot through my head in maybe three or four seconds, and when it was finished I was pretty sure that Kathy was right, except maybe for the part about concentrating and *trying* to make things conk out.

But I tried, and from the way her face looked, Mom was trying, too. As for Uncle Harold, I don't think he was listening, and I couldn't blame him, considering what was going on out in the kitchen where he was still lying on the floor.

Craystock had made it all the way into the kitchen by the time we started concentrating, and now he was knocking the cigarettes from Uncle Harold's mouth with a long stick he'd found somewhere. Uncle Harold was obviously doing his best to blow smoke toward the lizard, but Craystock was careful to keep upwind, and finally the cigarettes were on the floor and being shoved out the door with Craystock's stick. Out of sight in another part of the kitchen, some squeaky wheezing and some toenail clicking and scraping was going on, which I suppose meant the two kitchen lizards were recovering from the smoke Uncle Harold had puffed at them when he'd first burst in.

All our concentrating, however, didn't seem to be doing any good—or any harm, I guess I should say.

Probably everything that could be broken down already was. Dandelion's field-effect handcuffs were probably industrial strength or something and weren't affected by whatever we were doing.

If we really were doing anything besides scrunching up our faces and looking silly.

Actually, the only thing I was sure of was that we were making Craystock more nervous than he already was, which did not seem like the brightest thing in the world to do. For one thing, it looked like he had finally gotten things under control and was coming toward us with something in his hand that looked a lot like a gun, probably the same one that the assistant lizard had been pointing at us when Dandelion had knocked the invisibility gadget off him that first time.

But whatever it was, it was pointed at us, and Craystock was waving it back and forth like he couldn't decide which one to blast first.

15

"Stop Concentrating!"

"**C**raystock!" Dandelion hissed. "Do not be more of a fool than you already are!"

The lizard and his gun jerked to face Dandelion directly, and a series of harsh squeaks came from him, mixed with a jumble of more or less human sounds, but none of them English. There may've been a German or Spanish word or two in there somewhere, but it was hard to tell. Whatever was going on, however, it was pretty obvious that communication was out of the question unless his translation gadget started working again.

Then the two kitchen lizards poked their heads into the room and started squeaking, but Craystock cut them off with a screech that put my teeth on edge. I didn't think lizards could sweat, but this one was starting to look damp. And shaky. The way he was going, he could do us in by accident if he wasn't careful.

With his free hand, he jabbed frantically at one of the lumpy-looking things strapped to him, and then he squeaked some more. The sounds that came along with the squeaks were different from before, but they weren't any more understandable. A few of them were even sort of singsong like Chinese.

Meanwhile, I was still trying to move and getting nowhere, except for the same finger-wiggling I'd been managing for the last three or four minutes. I'm not sure what, if anything, the others were trying, but they obviously weren't having any better luck than I was.

But then, all of a sudden, it got easier. My whole hand could move.

And there was another voice, this one coming from the porch.

"Calvin!" it said, and it was almost as high-pitched as the lizard's voices. "Uncle Harold! Mommy! Where are you?"

It was Walter, of course.

"Come in here, Walter!" Dandelion called as loudly as she could. "Quickly!"

"No, Walter!" Mom cried suddenly. "Run! Get help!"

But Walter was already pushing the door open, and Craystock was squeaking frantically at the other two, one of which was toenail-clicking across the floor toward Walter. At the same time, Craystock did something to Dandelion's collar, still fastened around his wrist, and all of a sudden I could move my whole arm.

Walter saw the lizards and squeaked himself. "Mommy!" he screamed and ran pell-mell straight toward her.

Craystock stopped squeaking and fired the gun. Or I

guess that's what he did. At least he tried. He gave it a sort of squeeze, and it glowed for a fraction of a second, and then it hummed and sparked and smoked a little, and he dropped it like it had burned his fingers.

And at the same time—at the very instant Walter came tearing past Craystock, I swear—the field-effect handcuffs let go. I could move, and so could everyone else.

Dandelion moved the first and the fastest, faster than I'd ever seen even Hulk move. She landed on the chief lizard's arm, and a split second later she had her hands on the collar around his wrist.

Another split second and she had the collar off his wrist and on her own neck, and she was running for the door.

"Stop concentrating!" she hissed to us as she ran. "Stop concentrating before you destroy my entire ship!"

16

"What Was *Really* Going On?"

As it turned out, though, the concentrating probably didn't have anything to do with any of the breakdowns. At least not much. Which is only logical, once you think about it. I mean, in order to have some kind of effect, you have to know what you're concentrating on, and none of us had the foggiest idea when you got right down to it.

Later, using some of the confiscated Mildrolfan equipment as microchip guinea pigs, Dandelion figured out that it was the four of us—Mom, Uncle Harold, Walter, and me—all together in one spot that did most of the damage. Whatever we did to subatomic particles, we did a *little* of it when we were separate, enough to make any digital watches we wore break down after a few months, or to make Daschkor or Mildrolfan "bargain basement" equipment develop problems.

But when we were together, things really started

getting wild, especially when our emotions were all worked up. Or at least that's the way it seemed to work in Dandelion's experiments. Together, under a lot of stress, we made up some sort of critical mass. Sheriff Pippenger's watch, for instance, not even a digital one, stopped about the same time the outer-space stuff broke down. Without the stress, things still broke down around us, but not as much.

Anyway, when Dandelion dashed out the front of the house with her collar, the lizards all went dashing out the back, but before they got to where Craystock had left *his* ship, she'd gotten far enough away from the four of us to safely let the collar unfold into its ship form, so she was able to snatch them up without a lot of trouble. This time, with just the three of them to hold, her field-effect handcuffs worked just fine until she got them inside the ship itself.

Actually, the biggest problem could've been Sheriff Pippenger, but Dandelion was able to take care of that too. It was a sort of dirty trick, but when he went running out to his car to radio for reinforcements, she was able to pick it and him up, just like in the UFO magazines, and then put him down halfway across the county, where he stayed sound asleep in the car for three or four hours. As far as we know, he never said anything to anybody about the Diefenbacher place or the lizards or any of the rest of us. I guess he figured the whole thing was a nightmare, or maybe he was afraid he'd get laughed out of office if he started telling people about lizards from outer space just a couple of weeks after he'd told everybody there was a monster in that papier-mâché rock he'd tried to arrest.

As for Dandelion and everything else, it looked for a while like we weren't *ever* going to find out what had been going on.

When she got back to the Diefenbacher place from dumping Pippenger halfway across the county, all she did was ask for the invisibility gadget—which Kathy had grabbed from the floor sometime during the confusion—and Uncle Harold's detector, neither of which worked anymore. She didn't act like she was going to explain *anything*, at least not until Kathy practically yelled at her, "What was *really* going on? Why were those lizards here in the first place?"

When Dandelion hesitated even then, Uncle Harold said to her, "We saved your hide, don't forget that. No matter what you think, those scaly bozos were gettin' ready to wipe you out. And us."

She eyed the five of us for a second and gave her fur a riffle.

"Oh, very well," she said, and all of a sudden we were in her ship again, arranged in a sort of semicircle facing her as she floated in the air not far from where her miniature control panel had been before. Walter was the closest, and, finding himself almost on an eye level with her, he looked like he was coming very close to forgetting she wasn't a real cat. At least I could see his hand twitch now and then, like he was having trouble resisting an urge to reach out and pet her. As for the three lizards, they were in—yes, *in*—one of the walls, just barely showing through, kind of like three lizardy Frankenstein monsters in a plastic ice cave.

"That one," Dandelion said, pointing, "is Craystock. As I told you, he's their leader, such as he is. He sent them here to set things up, to 'buy' that out-of-the-way house."

"But what were they buying it *for?*" Kathy asked impatiently when Dandelion paused.

Dandelion riffled her fur again, this time probably in a sigh. "It was just another of his schemes," she said. "He's always doing something like that. The last time, on Elgmanac, he— But never mind. This time, basically, he was planning to set up a 'safe house' for criminals. His idea was that he would set up a tourist agency, but in every load of real tourists there would be a couple of outlaws who wanted to disappear for a while, until it was safe for them to return to civilization. They would just slip away from the others and stay behind. To tell the truth, I doubt that it ever would have worked, any more than his other schemes did, particularly when you look at those two squeaking lummoxes he was working with."

"Keep going," Uncle Harold prompted when she fell silent.

She gave him a look, but she continued. "Craystock sent those two ahead in their own ship to get the house set up while he worked at setting up the agency. The one assistant actually managed to buy the house, but then their equipment started breaking down. Your presence, Mrs. Willeford, may have caused some of the problems, but it wouldn't have taken much. By the time I arrived last week, about all that was working was the ship they had come in. Even their cloaking devices were working only part of the time."

"The invisibility gadgets," I put in.

"If you like," she said. "In any event, that is why the

so-called buyer of the house never showed up again. He was no longer able to take on a human appearance. To make sure they couldn't warn Craystock or cause any other trouble, I took their ship and hid it. That way, all they could do was stay in the house and wait for Craystock to arrive in his own ship."

She paused, giving Kathy and me a look. "Then you two arrived, talking as if you knew all about them. You frightened them, of course, and the first time you were there they locked you in that room. They were going to keep you there until Craystock came, but I used my restraining field to control them while I let you out."

"But why did you come back to my house with us?" I asked. "Why show yourself at all? Why not just stay where you were and wait for Craystock?"

Another fur riffle. "Perhaps I should have, but I was curious, and a little suspicious. You did, after all, talk rather much about aliens. And you were wearing that ring, something obviously not of Earthly origin. I simply wanted to be sure that you were not involved, either with Craystock or with some other group of whose existence I was unaware. And then, when I listened to you talking that evening about your 'Uncle Harold,' I recognized him and began to wonder if he had somehow been—corrupted, shall we say?"

Uncle Harold laughed. "You figured I'd found one of those characters you wanted me to watch for, only instead of telling you about it, I'd gone over to their side? And then recruited my nephew for some kind of skulduggery?"

"Behavior of that nature is not unknown to members

156

of your species, Hal, nor to other species on other worlds. In any event, I set up a series of devices that would alert me if a ship landed at the Diefenbacher house or at either of your houses. It was while we were reminiscing at your place in the country, Hal, that I was alerted to the landing of a ship back here. That is why I left in such a hurry. It was, of course, Craystock, but I apparently had underestimated him. He was gone when I arrived. I assume he spotted not only the detector I had set up here but the one at your place as well, Hal. That night, when the detector I had left at your place warned me that a ship had landed nearby, I went there immediately. Unfortunately, Craystock was ready for me, ready to snatch my ship away from me during its transition period." She riffled her fur more violently this time. "Not that it would have done him any good had my equipment not already been slowed by its proximity to the two of you."

"What about the ones that broke into our place?" I asked. "Were they looking for the invisibility gadget?"

"In all likelihood, yes, both times, but the second time it was Craystock who came, and he took your mother with him in hopes he could use her to force me to tell him where his assistants' ship was." She paused, and the purring sound she made sounded very much like a contented laugh. "The irony is, the ship was right in front of him the whole time. I had merely folded it as I do my own and placed it in a storage unit here in my own ship."

I'm not sure if Craystock was able to hear any of that, what with the way he and the others were submerged in the wall, but he did seem to change color a little.

"And that," Dandelion said, glancing around at the five of us, "would appear to be that. Now if you will excuse me, I am already long overdue back at headquarters."

And with that, we were all back on the ground, with the glow of her ship hovering a few feet away. All of us, that is, except Walter, who had been the closest to her the whole time she had been talking.

Mom, noticing he was missing, called his name loudly and started toward the glowing ship, but Uncle Harold put a hand on her arm.

"He'll be out in a second," he said with a grin. "Don't worry."

She gave him a puzzled frown, but she stopped.

"What's going on?" Kathy asked, sounding a little jealous. "Why's *Walter* still in there?"

Uncle Harold chuckled, looking at the glowing ship again. And as he watched, it faded into transparency, and Walter was standing on the ground beneath it, smiling.

And inside the ship, for just a second, we got a look at Dandelion. She was facing her control panel now, but for that second that we saw her, she didn't look like she was really paying a lot of attention to it. Instead, she had a look that I suddenly realized I'd seen on Hulk more than once, a sort of blissful look.

But then, as if pulling herself back to reality, she stiffened and darted one hand out toward the controls. An instant later, the glow became opaque and shot into the sky.

As the glow faded and vanished, Uncle Harold chuckled again and winked at Walter.

"Just remember, kiddo," he said, "no matter how scientific you get, you never outgrow the need for a good scratch behind the ears."